FRANKENSTEIN by Mary Shelley –

Adapted for Modern Readers

By Suparna Chakraborti

Frankenstein was first published in 1818 when Mary Shelley was twenty years old. Two hundred years later, the themes of humanity and scientific creation remain relevant for our modern society. Likewise, modern readers will recognize the human experiences, such as depression and physical deformity, which shape the characters and motivate their actions. Victor Frankenstein suffers from depression, and the 'creature' suffers rejection based on his physical appearance. Their personal experience is woven into the existential question – what makes us human?

for Mark
(1976-2018)

∞∞∞∞∞∞∞∞∞∞∞∞∞∞∞∞∞∞∞∞∞∞

Letter 1

St. Petersburgh, December 11th 17—
To Mrs. Saville, England

You will be glad to hear that nothing terrible has
happened. I know you were worried. I arrived yesterday, and
the first thing I am doing is writing to you - my dear sister
Margaret.

It is cold here in Petersburgh. The cold wind blowing on
my face makes me happy. Do you understand this feeling? This
wind comes from cold places. I imagine that the North Pole is a
beautiful place. Margaret - you can see the sun all day near the
North Pole. The explorers say the northern seas are calm. I
imagine that it is a wonderful place, and everything is possible
there. Maybe I can visit places that nobody has seen before. My
hopes conquer my fears. I feel as happy as a child setting off to
explore during his holidays. Even if I am wrong - it would be a
great thing to discover the passage through the northern seas.

I was feeling worried when I first started writing this letter.
Now I am filled with enthusiasm. I remember my purpose. I
have dreamed about this voyage since I was very young. I have
read about the voyages of other explorers to the North Pacific
Ocean. You might remember that our Uncle Thomas had many
books about explorers. I used to read his books day and night. I
used to regret that my father - before he died - told my uncle I
was forbidden to explore.

I forgot about exploring when I first read the great poets.
I spent one year trying to write poetry. I thought I could become
a great poet like Homer or Shakespeare. You know that I failed
- and you know how disappointed I felt. Just about that time, I

inherited some money from my cousin. I remembered my earlier dream to be an explorer.

I started planning for this voyage six years ago. I remember the exact hour when I decided I would take this trip. I began by making my body stronger. I joined whale-fishermen on several expeditions to the North Pacific Ocean where I endured cold, hunger, thirst, and lack of sleep. I worked harder than the common sailors during the day. During the nights, I studied mathematics, medicine, and physical science to help prepare for my adventure. I felt proud when my ship's captain offered to make me the second in command – and begged me to stay – because I did my work so well. I had enough money to live comfortably without working, but I preferred glory to everything else. Dear Margaret – don't I deserve to accomplish some great purpose? I wish I could hear some encouraging voice say – Yes! I am determined, but sometimes I feel discouraged. I am about to leave on a long and difficult voyage which will take all my strength. I will have to support my own spirits and other people as well.

This is the best time of year for traveling in Russia. We travel quickly over the snow in sledges, and the motion is pleasant. It is not too cold if you are wrapped in furs. I am wearing furs because it is colder sitting still in the sledge than working on the ship where you can stay active. I don't want to freeze on the way. I will stay in St. Petersburgh for two or three weeks – then I will go to the town of Archangel. I plan to hire a ship and sailors. I will sail in the month of June. When will I return? Dear sister – how can I answer this question? If I succeed – you might not see me for many months – or years. If I fail – you might see me soon – or never. Farewell – dear Margaret. I pray that Heaven will bless you – and save me – so that we might meet again. I am thankful for your love and kindness.

     Your loving brother – R. Walton

∞∞∞∞∞∞∞∞∞∞∞∞∞∞∞∞∞∞∞∞∞∞∞

Letter 2

Archangel, 28th March 17—
To Mrs. Saville, England

     The time passes so slowly here. I am surrounded by ice and snow. I have taken the second step towards my journey. I have hired a ship, and now I am hiring sailors. The sailors that I have already hired seem steady and brave.

     I do miss one thing very much, Margaret. I have no friend here to share my enthusiasm or disappointment. It is true I can write my feelings down on paper, but that seems like a poor way to share feelings. I would like to have the company of a friend who could share my adventure and help me stay balanced if I become too enthusiastic or impatient. Now I recognize the gaps in my education. Until I was fourteen, I read nothing but Uncle Thomas' books about voyages, and then I read the great poets. I have never learned other languages. I am twenty-eight years old, and many fifteen year old schoolboys know more than me. It is true that I have planned and daydreamed, but I don't have discipline. Well, it is useless to complain. I doubt that I will find a friend among the sailors and merchants. At the same time, I find some of the sailors are good men. My lieutenant has courage and ambition. He comes from England, and I first met him on a whale ship. Finding him unemployed in this city, I easily hired him for my adventure. My ship's master is a man of remarkable gentleness and strong character. I spent most of my childhood without companions – and I was guided by your gentle

3

influence. I dislike the brutal discipline on most ships. I feel very lucky to have a ship's master who is both kind-hearted and respected by the crew. I first heard about him through a romantic story. Some years ago, the master loved a young Russian lady. He saved his money, and then he asked the girl's father for permission to marry her. Her father agreed to the marriage. He met the girl once before the ceremony, and she cried and begged him not to marry her. She already loved a poor man, but her father would not agree to their marriage because the man was poor. The generous master released the girl from the marriage agreement. He had bought a farm, and he gave the farm and the rest of his money to the poor man so he could marry the girl. The girl's father tried to insist that she should still marry the master, but the generous master left the country until he heard the girl had married the man she really loved. You will say, "What a noble man!" It is true – but he is uneducated, and silent most of the time, and he can be careless – so it is hard to feel friendly toward him.

Just because I complain a little – I don't want you to think I am uncertain. I feel completely certain about my purpose, and I am only waiting for the weather to improve. We have had a severe winter, but it seems the spring might come early. I might sail sooner than I expected. You know I will do nothing without careful thought. I must be careful – since I am responsible for other men's safety.

It is hard to describe how I feel as my journey approaches. I can't put into words how excited and fearful I feel at the same time. I am going to places nobody has visited before. I work hard, and I am practical in my preparations for the journey. But, some poetic feeling pushes me to explore wild unexplored places. Remembering my dearest feelings – I wonder if I will meet you again after I sail around the world? I can hardly expect such success, but I am afraid to imagine failure. Please write to me whenever you have the chance. It is possible I will receive your letters when I need it most to support my spirits. I love you very much. Remember me fondly if you should never hear from me again.

Your loving brother, Robert Walton

∞∞∞∞∞∞∞∞∞∞∞∞∞∞∞∞∞∞∞∞∞∞∞∞

Letter 3

July 17th, 17—
To Mrs. Saville, England

My dear Sister,

I am writing to tell you I am safely on my way. I have met a ship traveling to England, and it will take this letter to you. I am feeling confident, and my men are bold. They are not discouraged by the floating sheets of ice that pass us from the north. We have come quite far north, but it is summer and the weather is warmer than I expected.

So far nothing has happened that is worth writing about. We have had one or two storms – and sprung a leak – but that is nothing for experienced sailors. I will be glad if nothing worse happens to us during this voyage.

Good-bye, my dear Margaret. I promise – for your sake and my own sake – I will not take chances. I will be calm, focused, and careful.

I feel certain we SHALL succeed. Why not? I have come this far over the unmarked seas. Why shouldn't I go further? What can stop a determined man?

My heart overflows – but I must finish this letter. Heaven bless my beloved sister.

R.W.

Letter 4

August 5th, 17—

To Mrs. Saville, England

Something strange has happened, and I can't help writing it down – though it is possible you will see me in person before you see this letter. Last Monday (July 31st) the ship was almost surrounded by ice with just a little clear space in front of us. The situation was somewhat dangerous, especially since we were surrounded by thick fog as well. We stayed in place hoping the weather would change.

The mist cleared away about two o'clock, and we saw vast sheets of ice stretching away in every direction. Some of my companions started to worry, and I was beginning to feel anxious myself, when we saw something strange that distracted us from our worries about our own situation. We saw a low carriage attached to a sledge, pulled by dogs, pass towards the north about half a mile away. A figure, which appeared to be a gigantic man, sat in the sledge and guided the dogs. We watched the traveler through our telescopes as he moved quickly over the ice until he disappeared from sight. We were astonished by this appearance. We had thought we were hundreds of miles away from land, but this figure suggested we were not as far from land as we had guessed. We could not watch him for long since we were enclosed by ice. About two hours later, we heard the ice begin to break, and before night our ship was free. We waited until morning to continue our journey, to avoid colliding with the floating masses of ice in the darkness, and I spent a few hours resting.

In the morning, I went up to the deck as soon as it was light. I saw the sailors over on one side of the deck talking to somebody below. During the night, a sledge had floated towards us, carried on a large block of ice. It was similar to the sledge we had seen earlier, but only one dog remained alive, and there was a human being sitting inside. The sailors were trying to convince him to come onto the ship. Unlike the other traveler, this man appeared to be European. When I appeared on the deck, the master said, "Here is our captain, and he will not let you perish at sea."

When he saw me, the stranger spoke to me in English, although he had a foreign accent. "Before I come on board," he said, "could you tell me where you are going?"

As you might imagine, I was astonished to hear this question from a man who was in such desperate circumstances. Our ship should have seemed like a priceless opportunity to him. I told him we were bound on a voyage of discovery to the North Pole.

My answer seemed to satisfy the man, and he agreed to come on board. Good God! Margaret – it would have shocked you to see this man who hesitated before accepting safety. Suffering and fatigue had made him incredibly thin, and his arms and legs were nearly frozen. I never saw a man in such terrible condition.

We tried to carry him inside the cabin, but he fainted as soon as we removed him from the fresh air. So, we carried him back to the deck and revived him by giving him a little brandy and rubbing his arms and legs with brandy as well. As soon as he began to show signs of life, we wrapped him in blankets and put him by the kitchen stove. Eventually, he felt strong enough to have a little soup, and then he seemed better.

It was two days before he could talk, and I was afraid that his suffering had damaged his mind. After his condition started to improve, I moved him to my own cabin and attended to him whenever I was not working. I never met a more interesting man. His eyes looked wild, even mad, but sometimes - after somebody had done him the smallest favor - he had the sweetest expression I ever saw. Most of the time he seemed depressed and discouraged, and sometimes impatient with the weight of the troubles that oppressed him.

When my guest started to recover, the men wanted to ask him a thousand questions, but I would not allow them to torment him with their curiosity. I knew that his recovery depended on total rest. One time the lieutenant asked him why he had come so far on the ice in such a strange vehicle.

His expression instantly became gloomy, and he replied, "I was seeking someone who ran from me."

"Did the man you followed travel the same way?"

"Yes."

"Then I think we saw him, because the day before we picked you up we saw some dogs pulling a sledge - with a man in it - across the ice."

This statement roused the stranger's attention, and he asked many questions about which direction the demon - as he called him - had gone.

Later, when we were alone, he said, "I am sure you, as well as your men, must be curious about my story, but you have been too considerate to ask me."

"I don't want to bother you with my questions."

"And yet - you rescued me from a strange and dangerous situation, and kindly restored me to life."

Soon afterward he asked if I thought the other sledge was likely to be destroyed when the ice broke up. I replied that I could not be sure because the ice had broken up after midnight, and the traveler might have reached a safe place by that time - but I was not certain. From this time onward, the stranger seemed filled with new energy. He was eager to be out on the deck watching for the sledge that had appeared before - but I persuaded him to stay in the cabin because he was still weak and the outdoors was extremely cold. I promised him that somebody would keep watch and call him immediately if something new appeared.

Such is my description of this strange event and what has happened up to this point. The stranger has gradually recovered his health, but he is silent, and he seems uneasy whenever anybody - besides me - enters the cabin. At the same time, his manners are so polite and gentle that the sailors are all interested in him, even though they interact with him very little. I have begun to feel like a brother towards him, and I am sorry to see his deep constant grief. He must have been a noble man in his better days, since he seems so attractive and appealing even in his shattered state. I told you in one of my letters, my dear Margaret, that I was not likely to find a friend on the wide ocean, but I have met a man I would have been happy to call my brother before his spirit was broken by misery.

I will tell you more about the stranger if something new happens.

August 13th, 17—

I feel more affection for the stranger every day. I admire him and pity him at the same time. How can I see such a noble man destroyed by misery without feeling sorry for him? He is so gentle, yet so wise, his mind is so educated, he speaks few words, yet his words are so quick and carefully-chosen. He has continued to recover from his illness and spends most of his time on the deck watching for the sledge that we saw earlier. He does not simply focus on his own unhappiness – although he is unhappy – he is interested in our work. I have talked with him frequently about my own project. He listened attentively when I described all the reasons I might succeed, and all the steps I had taken. He was so sympathetic that I did not hesitate to share the passion I felt for my purpose – and told him I would gladly sacrifice my fortune, my life, and all my hopes, to achieve my purpose. My single life was a small price to pay for the knowledge I sought, for the power I could give to the human race over the elements that oppose it. As I spoke, the stranger's face became dark and gloomy. At first I could see that he tried to control his feelings, then he placed his hands over his eyes, and I stopped speaking when I saw tears flowing from between his fingers. I paused, and he said brokenly, "Unhappy man! Do you share my madness? Has the dream made you drunk with its possibility? Hear me, let me tell you my story, and you will give up this dream!"

You might imagine that I felt curious when I heard his words, but his grief overcame his weakened state, and it required rest and hours of quiet conversation to help him recover. Once he regained control of himself, he seemed to feel disgusted with himself for losing control of his emotions. Setting aside his despair, he turned the conversation back to me and asked questions about my earlier years. It did not take long to tell my story, and talking about my early years reminded me how much I had always wanted to find a real friend. I expressed my belief that nobody could be really happy without the blessing of friendship.

"I agree with you," the stranger replied. "I think we are half-formed until somebody wiser and better than ourselves helps us improve our weak and faulty character. I once had a friend –

10

the noblest human creature – so I know something about friendship. You are young and have your whole life ahead of you, so you have no reason to despair. But – I have lost everything and cannot begin my life again.

As he spoke, his face expressed a calm, steady pain that moved me. He was silent and slowly returned to his cabin.

His spirit might be broken, but he still feels the beauty of nature deeply. The sight of the starry sky, the ocean, the views of this wonderful place, elevate his soul from earth. A man who loves nature lives a double existence. Even though he suffers and feels overwhelmed by disappointment, he is like a heavenly spirit surrounded by a halo where no grief can enter.

Do you smile at my enthusiasm for this wonderful stranger? You would not smile if you saw him. I know your refined nature would appreciate the extraordinary qualities of this man. Sometimes I wonder what quality seems to raise him so far above every other person I have known. I believe it is his penetrating intellect combined with the expressiveness of his face and voice which make his words sound like music to guide the soul.

August 19, 17—

Yesterday the stranger said to me, "I am sure you have guessed, Captain Walton, that I have suffered great misfortune. I had determined that the memory of this evil would die with me, but you have changed my mind. You seek for knowledge and wisdom, as I once did, and I hope your success does not destroy you as mine destroyed me. I do not know if my story will be useful to you, but I know you will be facing some of the same dangers that I faced. I think you might learn something that will help guide you if you succeed and console you if you fail. Prepare to hear things that will seem unbelievable. If I was telling you this story in some ordinary place, I might fear your

11

disbelief or ridicule. But, many things seem possible in this wild and mysterious part of the world where we can see the power of nature. Also, I expect the events will seem logical as I describe what happened.

As you might imagine, I was pleased by his trust, but I did not want him to become upset again by telling me his story. I told him that I was eager to hear the story he promised to tell, partly from curiosity and partly from the desire to help him if I could.

"I thank you for your kindness," he replied, 'but it is useless. My fate is nearly fulfilled. I wait for just one thing, and then I will rest in peace. I understand your feeling," he continued, seeing that I wanted to interrupt him, "but you are mistaken, my friend - if you will allow me to call you friend. Nothing can change my destiny. Listen to my story, and you will see how my fate has been determined."

He told me he would begin his story the next day whenever I had time to listen. I thanked him warmly for his promise. I have decided that every night, when I am not called away by duties, I will write down what he has told me during the day, as close to his own words as possible. Even if I am busy, I will make notes. I know that you will read this manuscript with pleasure someday. For me, knowing him and listening to the story from his own lips, I can only imagine the warmth and interest I will feel reading it later.

Even as I begin my task, I can hear his rich voice and see the melancholy sweetness shining n his eyes. I see him wave his thin hand as he speaks, while the expression of his face is brightened by the soul within. His story must be strange and terrible, he must have come through a frightful storm that has wrecked the life of a gallant man – this way!

∞∞∞∞∞∞∞∞∞∞∞∞∞∞∞∞∞∞∞∞∞∞

Chapter 1

I was born in Geneva, and my family is well-known there. My ancestors had served in the government for many years, and my father had held several public offices with honor. He was respected by everybody who knew him for his honesty and dedication to the public business. During his younger years, he was constantly occupied by government affairs, and he did not marry and become a husband and father until later in life.

I will tell you about the circumstance of his marriage because it reflects his character. One of my father's closest friends was a merchant named Beaufort who was once successful but fell into poverty through misfortune. Beaufort was a proud man, and it was difficult for him to continue living in the same country where he used to be wealthy and important. Beaufort paid his debts honorably, and then he moved with his daughter to the town of Lucerne where they lived in poverty and misery. My father loved Beaufort as a true friend, and it hurt him to see the change in his circumstances. He felt that Beaufort was motivated by false pride which did not allow him to accept help from his friends. My father wanted to offer Beaufort credit and assistance to help him begin his business again. Beaufort had hidden himself effectively, and it took my father ten months to find him. When he discovered their address, my father hurried to the house which was located on a poor street near the Reuss River. He found only misery and despair. Beaufort had saved just a little money from the wreck of his fortune, and it was enough to last for a few months. He had hoped to find some respectable work in a merchant's house. As the time passed, he became more and more overcome by depression, and by the end of three months he could not move from his bed.

His daughter cared for him with great tenderness, but she understood their money was running low, and they had no way to support themselves. Caroline Beaufort's uncommon courage and strength rose to support her during this difficult time. She found some plain work braiding straw and somehow managed to support herself and her father.

Several months passed this way. As her father grew worse, it required more time to care for him, and it became difficult for her to work. Ten months after they moved to Lucerne, her father died in her arms, leaving her with no money and no family. She knelt beside Beaufort's coffin weeping bitterly, when my father came into the room. He entered her life like a protecting spirit, and the poor girl immediately put herself into his care. After the burial, my father placed Caroline with a relative in Geneva. Two years later Caroline Beaufort became his wife.

The age difference between my parents only seemed to make them closer. My father could not love deeply unless he felt great respect as well. Perhaps he had loved somebody earlier in his life who had disappointed him, and now he placed great value on character. He was completely devoted to my mother, and his devotion and respect were based on her virtues. He wanted to make up for the sorrows she had suffered, and he did everything possible to protect her and bring her happiness. Her health and spirits had been shaken by her difficult experience. During the two years before their marriage, my father gradually gave up his public duties, and after they married my parents moved to Italy where the climate was pleasant, and the change of scene might be good for my mother's health.

From Italy they traveled to Germany and France. I was their oldest child, and I was born in Naples. I was their only child for several years. As devoted as they were to each other, my parents seemed to have limitless love to give to me. My mother's tender caress and my father's kind smile form my earliest memories. I was the focus of their lives – better than their plaything or idol – their child – my future happiness or misery was in their hands, and it was their duty to bring me up to

14

do good. My parents were deeply aware of their responsibility toward me - the being they had created – and they were motivated by love. While I learned lessons in patience and self-control as a young child, I was always guided by kindness. For a long time, I remained their only child, although my mother wished very much to have a daughter. When I was about five years old, my parents spent a week near Lake Como beyond the frontiers of Italy. Being kind people, they often visited the cottages of the poor. It was more than simple duty for my mother – it was a necessity and a passion – she never forgot how she had suffered, and how she was rescued, and she always did whatever she could to help the poor. During one of their walks, my parents noticed a small cottage in a valley with several poorly-dressed children gathered nearby. One day, when my father had gone by himself to Milan, my mother took me to visit this cottage. She met a hardworking peasant and his wife, bent by hard labor and worry, dividing a scanty meal among five hungry children. One child attracted my mother's attention more than the rest. The other four children were dark-eyed and strong, but this child was thin and very fair. Her hair was like bright living gold, and it seemed to crown her with special distinction in spite of her poor clothes. Her expression was untroubled, her blue eyes were bright, and her face and lips suggested sweetness. Nobody could look at her without feeling she was different from other beings, she had the stamp of heaven in all her features. The peasant woman noticed my mother admiring this lovely girl, and she eagerly told the child's history.

The girl was not her child, but the daughter of a nobleman from Milan. Her mother was German, and she had died giving birth to the child. The baby was placed with these good people to nurse. The peasant and his wife were not so poor at that time. They had not been married long, and their oldest child had just been born. The father of this little girl was one of those Italians who was fighting for the freedom of his country. He was imprisoned, and nobody knew whether he had died or he was still being held prisoner in Austria. His property was confiscated, and the child was left with nothing. The child continued to live with her foster parents, and she bloomed in their rough home like a fair garden rose among the brambles.

When my father returned home, he found me playing with this fair, radiant child whose movements were lighter than the antelope who lived in the hills. This vision was soon explained. With my father's permission, my mother asked the peasant couple to allow her to take charge of the child. The peasant couple was fond of this sweet child, and her presence had seemed like a blessing to them. They talked with their priest and decided it would not be fair to the child to keep her living in poverty when heaven had sent her this wonderful opportunity. The conclusion was that Elizabeth Lavenza came to live in my parents' home, and she became – more than my sister – the beautiful and beloved companion of all my activities and joys.

Everyone loved Elizabeth. I shared the feeling, and it delighted me that everybody who met Elizabeth seemed to have such passionate regard for her. On the evening before she came to live with us, my mother had said playfully, "I have a pretty present for my Victor – he will have it tomorrow." When she presented Elizabeth the next day as her gift to me, I took her words literally, being a child, and I believed that Elizabeth was mine – mine to protect, love, and cherish. When people praised her, I felt they were praising something that belonged to me. We called each other Cousin, but no word can describe my relation to her – more than my sister – until death she would be mine only.

∞∞∞∞∞∞∞∞∞∞∞∞∞∞∞∞∞∞∞∞∞∞∞

Chapter 2

We grew up together, and we were less than one year apart in age. Our relationship was harmonious, and the difference in our characters drew us closer together. Elizabeth was calmer and more focused, while I was more passionate, and I could work more intensely. I was more interested in gaining knowledge. She loved poetry and the beautiful scenes that surrounded our Swiss home – she found delight in the shape of the mountains, the changing seasons, the still winters, and the lively mountain summers. While Elizabeth admired the magnificent appearance of things, I delighted in studying the reason things happened. The world seemed like a puzzle that I wanted to understand. Some of my earliest memories involve curiosity, the desire to learn the hidden laws of nature, and my extreme joy when I learned something new.

When my parents had a second son, seven years after I was born, they gave up their wandering life and returned home to settle. We had a house in Geneva and a smaller home in the countryside where we spent most of our time. My parents enjoyed their quiet lifestyle. I never liked mixing with a crowd, instead I became closely attached to a few people. I was not interested in most of my classmates, but I became extremely fond of one friend, Henry Clerval, the son of a Geneva merchant. Henry was a boy of exceptional imagination and talent. He loved enterprise, hardship, and danger for its own sake. Henry enjoyed reading books about chivalry and romance. He wrote songs and stories about enchantment and heroic adventures. He tried to make us dress in costumes and act in plays where the characters were heroes and knights who fought against the infidels.

Nobody could have had a happier childhood. We never felt that our parents were trying to control us. Instead, we felt they were the source of everything good in our lives. When I visited other families, I realized how truly fortunate I was, and I felt gratitude as well as love for my parents.

By temperament I could be passionate and intense, but generally my passion was not directed towards childish interests but towards learning. I did not feel the same interest in all subjects. I will admit that I had no interest in languages, or government, or learning about the politics of different countries. I wanted to know about the outward reality of things and the inner spirit of nature - I was interested in the physical secrets of the world.

Meanwhile, Clerval was interested in the moral side of life. His focus was human society, heroic virtue, and the actions of men. He dreamed about becoming one of the gallant heroes who benefits humanity. Elizabeth blessed our home with her living spirit of love. My intense study might have made me moody, but her gentleness softened my intensity. And Clerval – could anything diminish the noble spirit of Clerval? Yet, through her influence, his passion for adventure was blended with generosity and the desire to help others.

I feel great joy when I recall the memories of my childhood, before misfortune had tainted my mind and turned my bright visions about the world into gloomy reflections about myself. Besides, when I describe my early days, I record the things that led step by step to later dark events. Science has ruled my fate, and I would like to describe the factors that led me to study science. When I was thirteen years old, we took a trip to the baths at Thonon, and we were forced to stay indoors due to the weather. I found a volume of the works of Cornelius Agrippa, and though I was not interested at first, I soon began reading with enthusiasm. When I went to my father to share my excitement, he looked at the little book and said carelessly, "Cornelius Agrippa – my dear Victor – don't waste your time. It is sad trash."

If my father had explained that modern theories of science had replaced the ancient principles of Agrippa, I would likely have returned to my earlier studies. But, my father had glanced at the book briefly, and I was not convinced that he knew about Agrippa. I continued reading with great interest. When I returned home, I ordered all the works of Agrippa, and then Paracelsus and Albertus Magnus. I read and studied their wild ideas, and it seemed they knew secrets known to few people besides myself. I have already said that I had a feverish desire to understand the secrets of nature. I appreciated the wonderful discoveries of modern scientists, but I always came away from my studies discontented and unsatisfied. It is reported that Sir Isaac Newton said he felt like a child picking up shells beside the ocean of truth. It seemed to me, even as a boy, that modern scientists were doing the same thing.

The uneducated peasant could look around and understand the practical uses of the elements around him. The most educated scientist understood little more. Science had partly unveiled the face of Nature, but her essence remained a mystery. The scientist might dissect and label, but he could not explain the ultimate cause of things. I was discouraged when I considered the barriers to understanding nature.

But here were books and men who claimed to understand much more. I took them at their word and became their disciple. While I was being educated in the schools of Geneva, I was largely self-taught with regard to my favorite subjects. My father did not understand science, and I was left to struggle by myself. I had the child's blindness combined with the student's desire for knowledge. Under the guidance of my new-found teachers, I began the search for the elixir of life, and the philosopher's stone that would turn metal to gold. I soon focused on the elixir, the potion to extend life. Wealth was unimportant compared to the glory I would achieve if I discovered the cure for age and disease. I had other visions as well. My favorite writers promised it was possible to raise ghosts and devils. My spells never succeeded, but I blamed the failure on my own mistakes rather than the books. For a time I floundered among multiple theories, guided by my passionate imagination and childish thinking, until something happened that changed my ideas.

When I was about fifteen years old, we were staying at our country house, and we witnessed the most violent thunderstorm. It came from the mountains, and the thunder seemed to burst from multiple places in the sky. I watched the progress of the storm with curiosity and delight. Standing by the door, I saw a stream of fire coming from a beautiful oak which stood twenty yards from the door. When the dazzling light disappeared, the oak was gone and nothing remained but a blasted stump. We found that the tree was not splintered but shattered into thin ribbons of wood. I had never seen something so completely destroyed.

I had known about electricity before, and a man who was interested in science was staying with us at the time. Excited by the catastrophe, he explained his theory about electricity and galvanism, and his explanation overthrew Cornelius Agrippa, Paracelsus, and Albertus Magnus, the writers who ruled my imagination. For some reason, I did not go back to my earlier studies. It seemed to me that nothing could or would ever be known. I felt disgusted with the subjects that had interested me for so long. Giving up my earlier thinking, I decided science was useless and would never lead to real knowledge. Instead, I turned to the study of mathematics as being more worthy of my attention.

Such small events shape our lives and bring us to prosperity or ruin. Looking back, I can see this move away from studying science to mathematics as my last chance to avoid the storm that was my fate. I felt unusually happy and calm after I gave up my old studies. I came to associate evil with the study of science through this experience - when I felt so happy without the scientific pursuit that had tormented me. Nevertheless, my fate could not be changed, and terrible and utter destruction would be my destiny.

Chapter 3

When I turned seventeen, my parents decided to send me to study at the University of Ingolstadt. Until then I had studied in the schools of Geneva, but my father wanted me to experience life outside my own country. I was preparing to leave when the first tragedy of my life occurred - maybe it was a sign of the misery to come. Elizabeth became severely ill with scarlet fever. During her illness, we convinced my mother to stay away from the sickroom. My mother agreed at first, but she could not control her anxiety when she heard that Elizabeth's life was in danger. My mother insisted on watching over the sickbed herself, and she saved Elizabeth with her watchful care. But, the consequences of this action were fatal for herself. My mother fell sick with the fever, her symptoms were alarming, and the doctor's expression suggested the worst outcome. She remained patient and strong even on her deathbed. She joined my hands with Elizabeth and said, "My children, my hopes for future happiness rested in your marriage. It will now bring happiness to your father. Elizabeth, my love, you must take my place with my younger children. I am sorry to be taken from you. I have known so much happiness and love, it is hard to leave you all. But – regret does not help. I will try to accept death cheerfully and hope to meet you in another world."

She died peacefully with a loving expression still on her face. I do not need to describe the darkness and despair of losing somebody you love to death. It takes time for the mind to accept that the person we saw every day is gone forever – the bright eye is extinguished and the familiar voice will never be heard again. The actual bitterness of grief begins after the first days have passed and the loss becomes permanent. Who has not lost somebody they love? Why should I describe sorrow which everybody has felt and must feel? The time comes when it is possible to smile again. My mother was dead, but we still had work to do, and we must continue to live and feel fortunate that we still had people to love.

The events had delayed my departure for Ingolstadt, and my father gave me permission to remain at home for a few more weeks. It seemed wrong to rush back into life. It was my first experience with grief, and I was reluctant to leave the people I loved. Most of all, I wanted to comfort my sweet Elizabeth.

She concealed her grief and tried to comfort us all. She accepted the duties of life with courage and determination. She devoted herself to the family she knew as her uncle and cousins. She had never seemed more enchanting than now, when she made herself smile so she could smile upon us. She forgot her own sorrow in her attempts to make us forget.

The day of my departure arrived. Clerval spent the last evening with us. He had wanted to come with me and study, but his father had not allowed it. His father was a narrow-minded businessman, and he considered his son's hopes and ambitions a waste of time. Henry deeply regretted not furthering his education. He did not say much, but when he spoke I saw shining in his eyes and face the determination not to be chained to the miserable details of business.

We stayed up late because we could not bear to leave each other or say the word "good-bye." We finally did say good-bye and retired to our rooms, pretending we were going to sleep, and when the dawn came they were all there again – my father to bless me again, Clerval to press my hand one more time, and Elizabeth to give her last attentions to her playmate and friend.

I threw myself into the carriage and reflected on the unhappy fact that I was alone for the first time in my life. At the university, I must make new friends and take care of myself. I had lived a sheltered life within my family, and I did not like meeting new people. I loved my brothers, Elizabeth, and Clerval, but I had no desire to mix with strangers. I began my journey with dark thoughts, but my spirits rose as I proceeded on

my way. I passionately wanted to acquire more knowledge.
While I had lived at home, I had often felt confined spending my
young life in one place. I had longed to see the world and take
my place in society.   Now I would have the opportunity, and it
was useless to think about regrets.

I had plenty of time for thinking since the journey to
Ingolstadt was long and tiring. At last, I could see the high white
steeple of the town. I descended from the carriage and went to
my rooms where I could rest.

The next morning I visited some of my professors.
Chance, or some evil influence, led me first to Monsieur
Krempe, professor of natural philosophy. He was uncouth but
knowledgeable about his science. He asked me several questions
about my previous scientific studies. My reply was careless and,
partly in contempt, I mentioned some of the writers I had
studied. The professor stared and said, "Did you really spend
your time studying such nonsense?"

When I answered – Yes - Monsieur Krempe continued,
"Every minute, every second, you spent studying those books was
wasted. You've filled your memory with useless terms and
disproved theories. Good God! Those books are one thousand
years old and completely outdated – how is it possible nobody
told you? I never thought I would meet a follower of Albertus
Magnus and Paracelsus in this modern, scientific age. My dear
sir, you must begin your studies anew."

He wrote down a list of several books about natural
science that he wanted me to read, and he told me he would be
giving a series of lectures about natural science starting the
following week, and Monsieur Waldman would be lecturing
about chemistry on the alternate days.

I had abandoned the writers I mentioned long ago, so
Monsieur Krempe's criticism did not bother me, but I did not
feel inclined to study natural science in any form. Monsieur
Krempe was a squat, unattractive little man with a rough voice,

and his appearance did not add to the appeal of his subject. I have described in detail the progress of my feelings about natural science. As a child, I was disappointed by the goals of modern scientists. The ancient scientists might be wrong, but they had grand vision, and they wanted to achieve power and immortality. Modern scientists had traded grand vision for knowledge about small details.

I spent the next two or three days becoming acquainted with the new place and people. The next week I remembered what Monsieur Krempe had told me about the lecture series. I could not bring myself to go hear his talk, but I recalled what he had said about Monsieur Waldman whom I had not met because he was out of town.

Partly from curiosity and partly from boredom, I went to the lecture room, and Monsieur Waldman arrived about the same time. He was very different from his colleague. He was about fifty years old with a kindly demeanor. His hair was mostly black with some gray around the temples. He was short but his posture was very upright, and he had the sweetest voice I had ever heard. He began his lecture by describing the history of chemistry, and he named the most distinguished scientists with enthusiasm. Next he gave the general overview of modern chemistry and explained the basic terminology. He showed some experiments, and then he finished with a statement about modern chemistry which I will never forget. "Ancient teachers promised impossible things, and they delivered nothing. Modern scientists promise very little because they know that metals cannot be turned into gold, and the elixir of life is a fantasy. But, modern scientists have performed miracles, even though it seems they spend their time looking into their microscope or crucible and getting their hands dirty doing experiments. They are uncovering the mysteries of nature. They rise into the atmosphere, they have discovered how the blood circulates, and the nature of the air we breathe. They have gained new and almost unlimited power – they command the thunder, create earthquakes, and even penetrate into the invisible world."

It seemed that my fate was preparing to destroy me through the professor's words. I felt as if my soul was struggling with some enemy. Every chord of my being was struck, and my mind was filled with one single purpose. Much has been done, the soul of Frankenstein exclaimed, but I will achieve far more, following in the footsteps already marked. I will pioneer a new way, explore unknown powers, and uncover the deepest mysteries of creation.

I did not sleep that night. My soul was in a state of turmoil and revolt. I knew that I would feel calm eventually, but I did not know how to calm myself. I fell asleep after the sun rose. When I woke, my thoughts from the day before seemed like a dream. The only thought that remained was my commitment to devote myself to my old studies. I felt that I had a natural talent for science. I visited Monsieur Waldman the same day. His private manners were even more appealing than his public personality. He seemed dignified while lecturing, but he was kind and pleasant in his own home. I described my previous studies to him as I had done with his fellow professor. He listened attentively and smiled at the names of Cornelius Agrippa and Paracelsus, but he did not criticize them. He said, "The enthusiasm of those men provided the foundation for modern scientists. They left us the easier task of naming and organizing the many facts they discovered. The work of men of genius benefits the world even when they are wrong." Without revealing my ambition, I told him that his lecture had changed my mind about modern chemistry, and I asked him which books I should read.

"I am happy to have gained a student," Monsieur Waldman said. "If your effort equals your ability, I am sure you will succeed. I have chosen the study of chemistry because it is the branch of science that had led, and will lead, to the most discoveries. But, I have not neglected the other branches of science. A good scientist will not focus on chemistry alone. If you really wish to become a man of science, and not just dabble with experiments, I would advise you to learn about every branch of natural science including mathematics." He took me into his laboratory and showed me his equipment, explaining what I should purchase for myself, and promising I could work with his equipment after I had learned to use it. He gave me the list of books which I had requested, and I left him.

So ended the day which decided my future destiny.

∞∞∞∞∞∞∞∞∞∞∞∞∞∞∞∞∞∞∞∞∞∞∞

Chapter 4

From this day onward, natural science, particularly chemistry in the broadest sense, became my sole occupation. I read books written by modern men of genius, I attended lectures, and cultivated the acquaintance of scientists at the university. I learned a great deal even from the lectures of Monsieur Krempe. His unattractive appearance and manners did not make his information and sound lessons less valuable. I found a true friend in Monsieur Waldham. His instruction was always given with frankness, good nature, and gentleness. He smoothed the path of knowledge in a thousand ways, and he made the most difficult topics clear and simple for my understanding. My effort was inconsistent at first, but my focus grew stronger as I continued, and soon I became so committed that night faded into morning while I was still working in my laboratory.

My hard work led to rapid progress. My commitment astonished the students, and my skill astonished the professors. Giving me a sly smile, Professor Krempe often asked how Cornelius Agrippa was doing, while Monsieur Waldman rejoiced to see my progress. I spent two years absorbed heart and soul in the discoveries I hoped to make, and I did not visit Geneva during that time. It is difficult to imagine the excitement of science unless you have experienced it. When you study other subjects, you go as far as others have gone before you, and there is nothing new to learn. Science involves the possibility of constant wonder and discovery. If you have reasonable ability and apply yourself with steady effort to one subject, you will eventually become expert in that subject. I devoted myself to the study of one subject with single-minded commitment, and I learned quickly. Within two years, I discovered ways to improve chemical instruments that won me respect and admiration at the university. By this point, I knew as much about natural science as my professors at Ingolstadt, and there was nothing new for me to learn by remaining at the university. I was thinking about returning to my home and family, when something happened which prolonged my stay.

I was particularly interested in the structure of living beings. What was the essence of life? It was a bold question, and the answer was generally considered a mystery. Yet, we are on the brink of knowing so many things if cowardice or carelessness does not restrict our curiosity. I decided to dedicate myself to the study of physiology. I would have found this study intolerable without my passionate interest. Learning about life meant I had to become acquainted with death. It was not enough to study anatomy, I had to learn about the decay of the human body after death. I was not raised to believe in superstition, and I was never afraid of darkness or ghosts. It did not bother me to reflect that bodies which used to be strong and beautiful became food for the worms after death. I spent days and nights in tombs and slaughter-houses studying the decomposition of bodies. I examined objects that other people would find impossible to consider. I learned how the fine human form decays. Death destroys beauty, and the worm consumes the wonders of the eyes and brain. I analyzed every detail involved in the change from life to death, and death to life, until suddenly light broke upon my darkness. I became dizzy with the immensity of my discovery. At the same time, it seemed so simple that I could not believe other men of genius had not discovered the secret before me.

Remember, I am telling you about facts and not about some madman's vision. The final discovery might seem like a miracle, but the result came from days and nights of tireless work. I discovered the ultimate cause of life, and I learned how to bring dead matter to life.

My first astonishment was replaced by rapture and delight. Obtaining my desire after so much painful effort was the most gratifying reward for my work. The discovery seemed so great and overwhelming that I forgot all the difficult intervening steps and considered only the final result. Since the beginning of time, wise men had dreamed of this discovery, and I had achieved it. Of course I did not accomplish my final goal all at once, but the discovery guided my pursuit.

I see by your eagerness, my friend, and the wonder and hope in your eyes, that you expect to learn my secret. I cannot tell you. Listen patiently until the end of my story, and you will understand why I cannot tell my secret. You are passionate and thoughtless as I used to be, I would not lead you to misery and destruction. Learn from my example, if not from my words, how dangerous knowledge can be. The man who thinks his small town is the whole world is happier than the man who wants to be greater than nature allows.

I hesitated for a long time considering how I should use the astonishing power I held in my hands. I had discovered how to bring dead matter to life, but preparing a body with its complicated fibers, muscles, and veins would be unimaginably difficult. I was uncertain at first whether I should attempt to create a being like myself or some simple creature. But, my initial success made me confident about my ability to create a being as complex and wonderful as man. My materials hardly seemed adequate for such a difficult project, but I had no doubt I would succeed. I prepared myself for setbacks, I knew that I would face challenges, and my work would be imperfect, but I knew how much progress happened every day in science and mechanics, and I hoped my attempt would lay the foundation for future success. I would not be discouraged by the scope and complexity of my project. With these feelings, I began the creation of a human being. The small size of the body parts slowed the speed of my work, so I changed my first plan and decided to make the being gigantic in size, about eight feet tall, and proportionately large. Having made this decision, and having spent months gathering my materials, I started work.

Nobody can imagine the variety of feelings that carried me onward like a hurricane in the first wave of my enthusiasm. I was going to break through the boundary of life and death and pour light into our dark world with my discovery. A new species would call me its creator. Many happy and excellent personalities would owe their existence to me. I would deserve their gratitude as completely as any father deserves the gratitude of his child. I had learned to bring dead matter to life, maybe someday I could renew life (though I could not do it yet) and bring dead beings back from their state of decay.

I pursued my project with the passion of complete commitment. The hours of study and confinement made me thin and pale. Sometimes I failed, when I seemed to be on the brink of achieving my goal, but I did not give up hope that the next day, or the next hour, might bring success. My hope rested on the secret that I alone possessed. The moon gazed on my nightly labor as I pursued nature in her hiding places. Who can imagine the horror of my secret work as I dug in the damp of new graves or tortured living animals so that I could bring life to non-living matter? My limbs tremble and my eyes blur when I remember my actions now, but some restless, frantic impulse drove me forward at the time. I seemed to lose all soul or sensation except for my one pursuit. Whenever the unnatural trance passed, I returned to my old habits with acute awareness of my condition. I collected bones from slaughter-houses, and my profane fingers disturbed the secrets of the human body. I set up my workshop of filthy creation in my solitary chamber at the top of the house separated from the other rooms by a hallway and staircase. Sometimes my eyeballs started from their sockets as I attended to the details of my work. I obtained most of my materials from the dissecting-room and the slaughter-house, and my human nature often felt loathing for my occupation, even while I felt increasing eagerness to reach my final conclusion.

31

The summer months passed as I pursued my work with single-minded purpose. It was a beautiful season, the fields and vines yielded the most plentiful harvest, but I was blind to the charms of nature. Just as I neglected the scenes around me, I neglected the family who was far away. I knew that my silence disturbed them, and I remember my father writing in his letter, "I am sure you will think of us with affection, as long as you are well, and we will hear from you regularly. You must excuse me if I conclude that you must be neglecting all your duties when we do not hear from you."

I understood how my father must be feeling, but I could not tear myself away from my work. It might be loathsome in itself, but it had taken irresistible hold of my imagination. I wanted to put my human affections on hold until I had achieved the great object which possessed me.

At the time, I felt my father was unjust if he thought my neglect came from some wrongdoing on my part. I now think he was correct to criticize my neglect. We should not allow passion or temporary desire to disturb our inner peace. I do not think the pursuit of knowledge gives us any excuse. If your study weakens your affections and appreciation for the simple pleasures of life, then your study should not be pursued, it is not worthy of the human mind. If people always followed this rule and did not allow any pursuit to disturb their human affections, Greece would not be enslaved, Caesar would have spared his country, America would have been settled gradually, and the empires of Mexico and Peru would not have been destroyed.

But, I am preaching morality at the most interesting part of my story, and your expression reminds me to continue. My father made no mention of my silence, and he only asked about my work in more detail than before. Winter, spring, and summer passed as I worked, but I did not notice the flowers or the growing leaves, which had always delighted me, I was so deeply involved in my project. The leaves had nearly withered before my work was complete, and now every day I came closer to the conclusion. But, my enthusiasm was mixed with anxiety, and I felt more like a slave doomed to work in the mines than an artist working on his favorite project. Every night I felt feverish, and I was painfully anxious, the noise of a falling leaf startled me. I avoided my fellow human beings as if I was a criminal. Sometimes I grew alarmed by the state of my health. The energy of my purpose was the only thing that sustained me. I told myself that my labors were almost over, and promised myself I could take a break as soon as my work was finished.

∞∞∞∞∞∞∞∞∞∞∞∞∞∞∞∞∞∞∞∞∞∞∞

Chapter 5

It was a dreary night in November when my project was accomplished. With painful anxiety, I collected the instruments I would use to give life to the lifeless thing that lay at my feet. It was already one o'clock in the morning, the rain pattered dismally against the window-panes, and my candle was nearly burnt out. By the half-extinguished light, I saw the creature open its dull yellow eyes, it breathed hard, and convulsively moved its limbs.

How can I describe my emotions at this catastrophe? How can I describe the wretch I had taken such painstaking care to create? His limbs were proportionate, and I had selected his features as beautiful. Beautiful! His yellow skin barely covered the muscles and arteries beneath, his hair was lustrous and flowing, and his teeth were pearly white. His shining black hair and white teeth formed a horrid contrast with his yellow watery eyes, his shriveled complexion, and his straight black lips.

Human feelings change quickly. I had worked hard for nearly two years for the sole purpose of giving life to a lifeless body. I had deprived myself of rest and health. My passionate desire had exceeded the bounds of moderation, but now that I was finished, the beauty of the dream vanished, and breathless horror and disgust filled my heart. I rushed out of the room, unable to stand the sight of the being I had created. I felt too agitated to sleep and continued to walk back and forth in my room for a long time. Eventually, fatigue overcame the turmoil I had experienced, and I threw myself down on my bed, still wearing my clothes, hoping to forget for a few moments. I slept, but I was disturbed by the wildest dreams. I thought I saw Elizabeth in the bloom of health, walking in the streets of Ingolstadt. Delighted and surprised, I embraced her, but as I kissed her lips, the color changed to the hue of death, and her features changed. I imagined that I held the body of my dead mother, she was wrapped in a shroud, and worms crawled in the folds of cloth. I woke from sleep in horror, my forehead was wet with cold sweat, my teeth chattered, and every limb quivered. By the dim, yellow light of the moon which came through the window-shutters, I saw the wretch - the miserable monster I had created. He held up the curtain of the bed, and his eyes looked at me. His jaws opened, he muttered some inarticulate sounds, and a grin wrinkled his cheeks. I did not hear if he spoke, I saw that one hand was stretched out towards me, but I escaped and rushed downstairs. I spent the rest of the night hiding in the courtyard, walking back and forth in great agitation, fearing that every sound marked the approach of the demoniacal corpse that I had brought to life.

Oh! No mortal being could stand looking at that face. A mummy brought back to life could not be as hideous as that wretch. I had gazed upon him while my work was unfinished, he had seemed ugly, but when those muscles and joints began to move, it became a thing even Hell could not have imagined.

I passed the night in misery. Sometimes my heart beat so quickly I felt the pulse in every artery. At other times I felt so weak I nearly sank to the ground from fatigue. Mingled with the horror, I felt the bitterness of disappointment as my pleasant dreams had instantly become like hell to me.

The wet, dismal morning dawned at last. My sleepless, aching eyes saw the white steeple and clock of the church of Ingolstadt which indicated six o'clock. The porter opened the gates of the courtyard where I had taken refuge for the night. I walked through the streets with quick steps as if trying to avoid the wretch whom I feared to see at every turn. I did not dare to return to my rooms, but felt impelled to hurry onward though I was drenched by the rain which fell from the gloomy, dark sky.

I continued walking for some time, trying to ease the weight which burdened my mind, with no clear idea where I was going or what I was doing. My heart throbbed with the sickness of fear and I hurried onward with uneven steps, not daring to look around me. I remembered some lines from Coleridge's "Ancient Mariner" -

>Like one who, on a lonely road,
>Doth walk in fear and dread,
>And having once turned round, walks on,
>And turns no more his head;
>Because he knows a frightful fiend
>Doth close behind him tread.

Continuing this way, I eventually reached the inn where carriages and vehicles usually stopped. I am not sure why but I paused here for some time and watched a carriage that was coming towards me from the other end of the street. As it came closer, I saw that it was a Swiss carriage. It stopped just where I was standing, and when the door opened I saw Henry Clerval. He sprang out as soon as he saw me. "My dear Frankenstein," he exclaimed, "I am so glad to see you! How lucky you should be standing here at the exact moment I arrive."

I was overjoyed to see Clerval. His presence reminded me of my father, Elizabeth, and memories of home. I grasped his hand and instantly forgot my horror and misfortune. I suddenly felt calm and serene joy for the first time in many months. I welcomed Clerval in the friendliest way, and we walked towards my college. Clerval continued talking for some time about our mutual friends and his good fortune to be allowed to come to Ingolstadt. "You can imagine," he said, "how much difficulty I had convincing my father that book-keeping is not the only subject worth knowing. I don't think I actually convinced him, because he kept repeating that education had never affected his income, but his affection for me eventually overcame his dislike of learning. He has allowed me to come to the university."

"I am delighted to see you - tell me, how are my father, brothers, and Elizabeth?"

"Very well and very happy – except they worry because they rarely hear from you. I am going to lecture you myself – but, my dear Frankenstein," he said, stopping and gazing at my face, "I did not notice at first you look so ill, you are pale and thin, it seems you have not slept for many nights."

"You have guessed rightly. I have been working so hard recently, I have not allowed myself to rest. But, I am hoping that my work is finally finished, and I will be free."

I trembled because I could not bear to think about the events of the night before, much less talk about them. I walked quickly, and we soon arrived at my college. I now reflected that the creature, whom I had left in my rooms, might still be there. I dreaded to see the monster, but I feared still more that Henry should see him. I asked Henry to wait for a few minutes and darted up the stairs to my own room. My hand was on the lock of the door before I paused and felt cold shivering come over me. I opened the door forcefully, as children do when they expect that something might be waiting on the other side, but nothing appeared. I stepped inside fearfully and discovered the room was empty. My bedroom was also free of its hideous guest. I could hardly believe my good luck, and when I felt sure my enemy had left, I ran joyfully down to Clerval.

We walked upstairs to my rooms, and the servant brought us breakfast, but I had difficulty controlling myself. It was not just joy that possessed me. My flesh seemed to tingle, and my heart beat rapidly. I could not remain in one place. I walked around the room, jumped over chairs, clapped my hands, and laughed out loud. At first, Clerval thought I was overjoyed by his arrival, but when he looked more closely he saw wildness in my eyes, and my loud, unrestrained, heartless laughter surprised and frightened him.

"My dear Victor," he cried, "what is the matter? Don't laugh that way! You're not feeling well – What is the cause for all this?"

37

"Don't ask me," I cried, putting my hands over my eyes. I thought I saw the dreaded specter glide into the room. "HE can tell. Oh save me! Save me!" I imagined that the monster seized me. I struggled furiously and fell to the floor in a fit.

Poor Clerval! What did he feel at that moment? He had looked forward to our meeting with such joy, and it had turned so strangely into bitterness. But, I was not aware of his grief, because I was unconscious, and I did not recover my senses for a long, long time.

It was the beginning of a fever that affected my nerves and lasted for several months. Henry was my only nurse during all that time. I learned afterward that he spared my father and Elizabeth the news. He knew my father's advanced age made the long journey difficult for him, and Elizabeth would worry if she knew about my sickness. Henry realized that I could not have a kinder, more attentive nurse than himself, and he did not doubt my ultimate recovery. He felt that he was doing the kindest thing possible for my father and Elizabeth.

But, I was very ill, and only the constant attention of my friend could have saved me. I imagined that I saw the monster I had created, and I raved about him incessantly. I am certain that my words surprised Henry. He must have thought I was delirious at first, but my persistence in talking about the same subject convinced him that my sickness was caused by some terrible event.

I recovered slowly, with frequent relapses that alarmed my friend. I can remember when I first started noticing things with enjoyment again. I saw that the fallen leaves had disappeared, and the trees that shaded my window were sprouting young buds. It was a beautiful spring, and the season contributed to my recovery. My gloom disappeared, and I felt joy and affection revive in my heart. Within a short time, I became as cheerful as I was before the fatal passion attacked me.

"Dearest Clerval," I exclaimed, "you are so kind and good to me. You came here to study and instead you have spent the whole winter consumed by my sickness. How can I ever repay you? I am so sorry to give you trouble, but I know you will forgive me."

"You can repay me completely if you get well as soon as you can, and do not make yourself upset. Since you seem to be feeling better, I may speak to you about one subject – may I not?"

I trembled. One subject! What could it be? Could he mean the object I could not bear to think about? "Don't worry," Clerval said, "I won't mention it, if it bothers you, but your father and cousin would be very happy to get a letter from you in your own handwriting. They didn't know you were so ill, and they are worried by your long silence."

"Is that all, my dear Henry? Of course - I should think first about the family that I love."

"Since you feel that way, you might be glad to see the letter that came for you several days ago. I believe it is from your cousin."

Chapter 6

Clerval put the following letter into my hands. It was from my own Elizabeth.

"My dearest Cousin,

You have been ill, very ill, and even dear, kind Henry's letters do not convince me that you are improving. You are not allowed to write, dear Victor, but we need one line from you to ease our worry. For a long time, I have thought each letter would bring some word from you. I have persuaded my uncle not to make the journey to Ingolstadt. I knew he would face inconvenience and perhaps danger making such a long journey, yet I have often regretted that I could not go myself. I imagined that some old nurse was caring for you, and she could never guess your wishes or care for you with the affection of your poor cousin. But, I am finished worrying now. Clerval says you really are improving. I hope you will confirm his news soon in your own handwriting.

Get well - and return to us. You will find a happy, cheerful home and friends who love you dearly. Your father is healthy and strong. Nothing can disturb his happiness as long as he can see you, and knows that you are well. You would be pleased to see how much our Ernest has grown! He is now sixteen and full of activity and spirit. He wants to be a true Swiss and enter the foreign service, but we cannot let him go, at least until his older brother returns to us. My uncle is not pleased with the idea of Ernest having a military career in a faraway country, but Ernest never had your talent for study. He thinks studying is a waste of time, and he prefers to be outdoors climbing the hills or rowing on the lake. I fear he will become lazy if we do not agree and allow him to enter the profession he has chosen.

Nothing has changed since you left, except the dear children have grown. The blue lake and the snowy mountains, they never change, and I think our peaceful home and contented hearts follow the same laws. My small occupations take up my time and keep me amused. My work is rewarded by seeing only happy, kind faces around me. One change has taken place since you left us. Do you recall when Justine Moritz came to our family? You might not remember, so I will tell you about her history in a few words. Her mother, Madame Moritz, was a widow with four children, and Justine was her third child. Justine was her father's favorite, but her mother had always hated her. After Monsieur Moritz died, Justine's mother treated her very badly. When Justine was twelve years old, my aunt asked her mother if she could come live at our house. The manners of the different classes are not so distinct in our country. The poor are not so despised here, and the lower classes are more refined and moral. Being a servant in Geneva does not mean the same thing as being a servant in France and England. Justine came to live with our family as a servant, but she kept her dignity as a human being.

You may remember, Justine was always a great favorite of yours. I recall you once remarked that if you were ever in a bad mood, one glance from Justine could cure it because she looked so open-hearted and happy herself. My aunt grew very fond of Justine and made sure she was educated. Justine repaid her by being the most grateful little creature in the world. I do not mean she talked about being grateful, but she looked at my aunt with adoration in her eyes. Although she was light-hearted, and careless in many ways, she was attentive to my aunt's every gesture. She thought my aunt was the model of excellence, and she tried to imitate her phrases and manners. Even now, Justine often reminds me of her.

When my dearest aunt died, everybody was too absorbed in their own grief to notice Justine. She had cared for my aunt during her illness with anxious affection. Poor Justine became very ill, but more misfortune followed.

One by one, her brothers and sister died, and her mother was left childless except for her one neglected daughter. Justine's mother began to think that the loss of her favorite children was punishment because of her partiality for them. She was Roman Catholic, and I think her priest supported this idea. Accordingly, a few months after you left, Justine's mother summoned her home. The poor girl wept when she left our house. She had changed after my aunt died. Grief had made her manners soft and mild, when she had been lively before. Her stay at her mother's house was not likely to improve her spirits. Her mother's behavior towards her varied widely. She sometimes begged Justine to forgive her for her unkindness, but more often she scolded Justine for causing the deaths of her brothers and sister. Constant fretting threw Madame Moritz into a decline, which made her more irritable at first, but now she is at peace forever. She died at the beginning of this past winter just before the cold weather came. Justine has just returned to us, and I must tell you that I love her dearly. She is very clever and gentle, and extremely pretty. As I mentioned before, her expression and manners constantly remind me of my dear aunt.

My dear cousin, I must say a few words about little darling William. I wish you could see him. He is tall for his age with curly hair, sweet laughing blue eyes, and dark eyelashes. When he smiles, he has two little dimples on each rosy cheek. He has already had one or two little WIVES, but Louisa Biron is his favorite – she is a pretty little girl about five years old.

Now, dear Victor, I would guess you do not mind hearing a little gossip about the good people of Geneva. The pretty Miss Mansfield is engaged to a young Englishman, John Melbourne, Esq. Her ugly sister, Manon, married a rich banker last autumn. Your favorite classmate, Louis Manoir, has had several misfortunes since Clerval left Geneva. But, he has already recovered his good spirits, and he is about to marry a lively, pretty Frenchwoman, Madame Tavernier. She is a widow, and she is much older than Manoir, but she is much admired and popular with everyone

I have written myself into better spirits, dear cousin, but I feel anxious again as I conclude this letter. Write, dearest Victor, one line – one word – will be a blessing to us. Ten thousand thanks to Henry for his kindness, his affection, and his many letters we are sincerely grateful. Good-bye, my cousin, take care of yourself, and I beg you, write!

Elizabeth Lavenza

Geneva, March 18, 17–"

"Dear, dear Elizabeth!" I exclaimed, when I had read her letter. "I will write to them right away and relieve their anxiety." Writing tired me, but my recovery had begun. After two weeks, I was able to leave my rooms.

One of my first duties following my recovery was introducing Clerval to the professors at the university. The introductions involved some difficulty for me after the stress my mind had sustained. Even since the fatal night when my project was finished and my misfortunes began, I had developed a hatred for science. Even when I seemed completely recovered, the sight of a chemical instrument would renew the agony of my nervous symptoms. Henry had noticed my distress, and he had removed all of my equipment from view. He had also changed my rooms, sensing how much I disliked the room that used to be my laboratory. But, Henry could not protect my feelings when I visited the professors. Monsieur Waldman tortured me with his warm, kind praise about the astonishing progress I had made in the sciences. He soon realized that I disliked the subject, but he did not guess the real reason. Supposing I was motivated by modesty, he changed the subject from my progress to the science itself, trying to involve me in the conversation. What could I do? He was trying to please me, and he tormented me. I felt as if he was laying out, one by one, the cruel instruments that would be used to put me to death. I writhed when I heard his words, but I could not express the pain I felt. Clerval was always sensitive to the feelings of others. He claimed to be completely ignorant of science, and the topic of conversation became more general. I thanked my friend from my heart, but I did not speak. I could see clearly that he was surprised, but he never asked about my secret. I loved and respected Henry more than I could say, but I could not bring myself to tell him about the event that lived in my memory. I was afraid that talking about the subject would only make it more vivid in my mind.

Monsieur Krempe was never polite. In my state of extreme sensitivity, his harsh, blunt praise gave me even more pain than the milder praise of Monsieur Waldman. "Damn the fellow!" he cried. "I can assure you, Monsieur Clerval, he has outstripped us all. Stare if you like – it is true. The same youngster who believed in the literal truth of Cornelius Agrippa, now he is the best scholar in the university. If we don't take him down a little bit, we will all be displaced. I know Monsieur Frankenstein is modest," he continued, noticing the suffering expression on my face, "and modesty is an excellent quality in a young man. Young men should be modest about themselves. You know, Monsieur Clerval, I was modest myself when I was young, but you soon get over that."

Monsieur Krempe now began a speech in praise of himself, which fortunately turned the subject of conversation away from me.

Unlike me, Clerval was interested in literature rather than science. He had come to the university hoping to master the Eastern languages and prepare himself for a glorious career in the East. He focused on the Persian, Arabic, and Sanskrit languages, and I was easily persuaded to join him. I had come to hate my former studies, but I never liked being idle, and it was a great relief to join my friend in his studies. I found not only instruction but consolation in Eastern literature. I did not try to become completely familiar with the languages, as Clerval did, I simply read for meaning, and my effort was well rewarded. The sadness was soothing, and the joy lifted me higher than the writing of any other country. When you read this literature, life seems to consist of warm sun and rose gardens – the smiles and frowns of your fair enemy - and the fire that consumes your own heart. How different from the manly, heroic poetry of Greece and Rome!

Summer passed in this way, and my return to Geneva was fixed for late autumn. My departure was delayed by several accidents, and winter came with snow that made the roads impassable. I was bitterly disappointed to find my journey delayed until the following spring. I longed to see my native town and my beloved family. I had only stayed because I was reluctant to leave Clerval until he became acquainted with the new place. We spent the winter cheerfully. Spring came late, but its beauty made up for its lateness.

The month of May arrived, and I expected to receive the letter fixing my departure any day. Henry suggested that we should take a walking tour of the region surrounding Ingolstadt, so I could say farewell to the place where I had lived for so long. I agreed to his suggestion with pleasure. I enjoyed exercise, and Clerval was always my favorite companion for the walking tours I had taken at home.

We spent two weeks rambling through the country. I had long since recovered my health and spirits, and I felt even stronger as I breathed the healthful air, walked through the natural scenery, and talked with my friend. Study had kept me separated from my fellow creatures, but Clerval revived the better feelings of my heart. He reminded me to love nature and the cheerful faces of children. Excellent friend! How sincerely you loved me and tried to lift my mind up to your own level. My

selfish pursuit had cramped and narrowed my thinking, until
your gentle influence and affection warmed my senses.   I
became the same happy person I had been a few years before
when I had no sorrow or care, and everybody loved me. When I
am happy, nature fills my mind with the most delightful
sensations. The serene sky and green fields filled me with
ecstasy. The season was truly divine. Spring flowers bloomed in
the hedges, and summer flowers were already budding. I was
undisturbed by the thoughts that had weighed me down the year
before no matter how much I had tried to push them away.

      Henry rejoiced when he saw me so happy. He did his
best to amuse me, and he shared the thoughts that filled his soul.
The creativity of his mind was truly astonishing, and his
conversation was filled with imagination. Imitating the Persian
and Arabic writers, he made up stories of wonderful fancy and
passion. At other times, he recited my favorite poems, or
involved me in arguments that he supported with great
cleverness. We returned to our college on a Sunday afternoon
when the peasants were dancing and everyone we met seemed
gay and happy. My heart felt light, and I bounded along with
unfettered joy and happiness.

∞∞∞∞∞∞∞∞∞∞∞∞∞∞∞∞∞∞∞∞∞∞∞
Chapter 7

When I returned home, I found the following letter from my father:

"My dear Victor,

No doubt you have waited impatiently for a letter fixing the date of your return to us. At first I was tempted to write a few lines and just tell you the date. But, that would be a cruel kindness and I cannot do it. I imagine your shock, my son, when you arrive expecting a happy welcome, and we meet you with tears and wretchedness. Victor, how can I tell you about our misfortune? I am sure absence has not made you indifferent to our joys and sorrows. How can I give pain to my long absent son? I wish I could prepare you to hear the sad news, but I know it is impossible. I am sure you are already skimming through my letter to find the words which will tell you the horrible news.

William is dead! - The sweet child who delighted me with his smiles and warmed my heart, who was so gentle, yet so joyful! Victor, he is murdered!

I will not try to comfort you, I will simply tell you what happened.

Last Thursday (May 7th) I went for a walk in Plainpalais with my niece and your two brothers. The evening was peaceful and warm, and we walked farther than usual. It was already dusk before we decided to turn back, and then we could not see William and Ernest who had gone ahead. We rested on a seat waiting for them to return. After some time, Ernest came back and asked if we had seen William. He had been playing with his brother, and William had run away to hide himself. Ernest had looked for him, and he had waited for a long time, but he had not returned.

His story alarmed us, and we continued to search until night fell, and Elizabeth suggested he might have returned to the house. He was not there. We returned again with torches. I could not rest when I imagined my sweet boy lost and exposed to the damp night. Elizabeth suffered from extreme anxiety as well. About five in the morning, I found my lovely boy, who was blooming and healthy the night before, stretched pale and motionless on the grass. The murderer's fingerprints were visible on his neck.

We carried him home, and Elizabeth guessed what had happened when she saw the expression on my face. At first I tried to prevent her, but she insisted on seeing the body. Going into the room, she quickly examined the victim's neck, clapped her hands, and exclaimed, "O God! I have murdered my darling child!"

Elizabeth fainted, and we revived her with great difficulty. When she regained consciousness, she could only weep and sigh. She told me that William had begged her just that evening to be allowed to wear a very valuable miniature of your mother that belonged to Elizabeth. The picture was gone, and it had doubtless tempted the murderer to do this deed. We continue to search, but we have found no trace of the murderer, and it will not restore my beloved William!

Come home, dearest Victor, you are the only person who can comfort Elizabeth. She weeps constantly and accuses herself unfairly of his death. Her words pierce my heart. We are all miserable, but perhaps that will motivate you more, my son, to return and comfort us? Your dear mother! Alas, Victor! I thank God now that she did not live to see the cruel, miserable death of her youngest darling.

Come, Victor, do not dwell on brooding thoughts of revenge against the murderer. Bring feelings of peace and gentleness to help heal the wounds of our minds instead of increasing them. Enter the house of mourning with kindness and affection for the people who love you, and not with hatred for your enemies.

Your affectionate and suffering father,
Alphonse Frankenstein
Geneva, May 12th, 17—"

Clerval was surprised to see my expression change from joy to despair as I read this letter. I threw the letter on the table and covered my face with my hands.

"My dear Frankenstein," Henry exclaimed when he saw me weeping bitterly, "must you always be unhappy? My dear friend, what has happened?"

I gestured for him to take the letter while I paced back and forth in extreme agitation. Clerval's eyes overflowed with tears as he read the news

"I can say nothing to console you, my friend," he said, "nothing can make up for your loss. What do you plan to do?"

"I will go to Geneva right away, Henry, come with me to order the horses."

Clerval tried to comfort me as we walked. He could only express his heartfelt sympathy. "Poor William!" he said, "dear, lovely child. He sleeps with his angel mother now. Everyone who knew his bright, joyful young beauty must weep for his untimely loss. What kind of murderer could destroy such radiant innocence? Poor little fellow! Our only comfort is knowing that he is at rest. His suffering is ended forever, and he feels no pain. We must save our pity for his miserable survivors."

Clerval spoke as we hurried through the streets, and I remembered his words later when I was alone. But now, I said farewell to my friend and hurried into the carriage as soon as the horses arrived.

My journey was very melancholy. At first, I wanted to hurry onward so that I could comfort and sympathize with my sorrowing family. But, I slowed my pace when I came near to my native town. I could barely contain the multitude of feelings that crowded into my mind. I passed through places I had known in my youth, but had not seen for nearly six years. How many things might have changed during that time! One sudden, terrible change had taken place, but a thousand more gradual changes might have happened which might be just as significant. I was overcome by fear and did not dare to go forward. I dreaded a thousand nameless evils that made me tremble though I could not name them. I remained in Lausanne for two days in this painful state of mind. I gazed at the calm waters of the lake and the snowy mountains which had not changed. The calm, beautiful scenes gradually restored me, and I continued my journey to Geneva.

The road ran beside the lake, and it became narrower as I approached my nature town. I observed the mountains more closely and wept like a child. "Dear mountains! My own beautiful lake! How do you welcome your wanderer? Your summits are clear, and the sky and lake are tranquil and blue. Do you predict peace, or do you mock my unhappiness?"

I am afraid, my friend, I will bore you with this introduction to later events, but I still felt some happiness in those days, and I remember them with pleasure. My country, my beloved country! Who else but a native could understand the delight I felt when I saw your streams, and mountains, and your lovely lake.

Yet, fear and grief overcame me again as I came close to home. Night fell around me, and I felt gloomy when I could no longer see the mountains. I seemed to be surrounded by a vast and dim scene of evil. I looked into the future and saw myself destined to become the most wretched of human beings. Alas! My prediction came true. I only failed to guess that my misery and anguish would be one hundred times greater than I imagined. It was completely dark when I arrived in Geneva, and the gates of the city were already shut. I was forced to spend the night at Secheron, a village outside the city. The sky was clear, and I could not rest. I decided to visit the spot where my poor William was murdered. Since I could not pass through the city, I had to cross the lake in a boat to reach Plainpalais. During the short voyage, I saw lighting making beautiful patterns around the summit of Mont Blanc. The storm moved quickly. I climbed a low hill after I landed so that I could watch its progress. I soon felt the rain falling in large drops, clouds filled the sky, and the violence of the storm increased rapidly.

I left my seat and walked forward, although the darkness and storm increased every minute, and thunder burst with terrific noise over my head. The crash of thunder echoed from the mountains, and vivid flashes of lightning dazzled my eyes, lighting up the lake and making it look like a vast sheet of fire. Between the flashes of lightning, everything seemed to be pitch darkness until my eyes recovered from the dazzling light. The storm seemed to come from various parts of the sky, as happens in Switzerland. The most violent part of the storm hung exactly north of the city, while smaller storms darkened the surrounding mountains.

While I watched the tempest – so beautiful yet terrible – I walked forward with rapid steps. The war in the sky lifted my spirits. I clasped my hands and exclaimed out loud, "William, dear angel, this is your funeral, this is your lament!" As I said the words, I saw a figure in the gloom step out from behind a clump of trees nearby. I stood still and gazed intently. I could not be mistaken. A flash of lighting illuminated the object and showed me its shape clearly. It was gigantic in size, and no human face could be so hideous. I instantly recognized the wretch, the filthy demon I had created. What was he doing there? I shuddered when I considered – whether he might be the murderer of my brother? As soon as I imagined this possibility, I became convinced it was the truth. My teeth chattered, and I leaned against a tree for support. The figure quickly passed me, and I could not see it in the darkness.

HE was the murderer. I did not doubt that he had destroyed the fair child. The mere idea seemed to prove the fact. I thought of going after the devil, but it would have been useless, because the next flash showed him climbing up the vertical mountainside. He soon reached the summit and disappeared.

I remained motionless. The thunder stopped, but the rain continued, and I was surrounded by impenetrable darkness. I thought about the events I had tried so hard to forget. I recalled my progress toward the moment of creation, the appearance of the creature at my bedside, and its disappearance. Almost two years had passed since the night when I first gave it life. Was this its first crime? Alas! I had set this depraved wretch loose in the world, and he seemed to delight in carnage and misery. Had he not murdered my brother?

Nobody can imagine the anguish I felt during the remainder of the night. I stayed outside, cold and wet, but I scarcely felt the weather. I imagined scenes of evil and despair. I considered the being whom I had released among mankind. I had given it the will and power to pursue horrible deeds. He seemed to be my own spirit let loose from the grave and forced to destroy everything that was dear to me.

Dawn came, and I walked toward the city. The gates were open, and I hurried to my father's house. My first thought was to share what I knew about the murderer and instantly begin pursuit. But, I paused when I considered the story I had to tell. A being that I myself had created, and endowed with life, had met me at midnight among the mountains. I remembered the nervous fever I had suffered just following its creation. My story would seem to be rooted in delirium, it was so utterly unbelievable. I knew that if somebody told me this story, I would think he was insane. Even if I could persuade my relatives to begin the search, I felt sure the creature would escape. So, what was the use of chasing him? Who could capture a creature which could climb up the sheer side of a mountain?

It was about five o'clock in the morning when I reached my father's house. I told the servants not to disturb the family, and I went into the library to wait for them to rise.

Six years had passed like a dream - except for one thing I could not erase. I stood in the same place where I had last embraced my father before I left for Ingolstadt. I remembered my respected and beloved father. I gazed at the picture of my mother which hung over the mantel piece. My father had ordered the painting, and it showed Caroline Beaufort kneeling beside her dead father's coffin. Her clothes were simple, and her face was pale, but her expression of dignity and beauty did not allow pity. Below this picture was a miniature of William, and my tears overflowed when I looked at it. Ernest had heard me arrive, and he now came into the room. "Welcome, my dearest Victor," he said. "Ah! I wish you had come three months ago, and you would have found us happy and delighted to see you. Now you have come to share this misery which nothing can change. Yet, I hope your presence will help revive Father. He seems to be sinking under this misfortune. And, I hope you can persuade poor Elizabeth to stop blaming herself. Poor William! He was our darling and our pride!"

My brother wept without restraint, and a feeling of mortal agony crept over me. Before, I had only imagined the desolation of my home. The reality struck me as a new and terrible disaster. I tried to calm Ernest, and asked about my father and Elizabeth in more detail.

"She requires comfort most of all," Ernest said. "She accuses herself of causing my brother's death, and it makes her miserable. But, since we have found the murderer - "

"You have found the murderer! Good God! How can that be? Who could attempt to pursue him? It is impossible!

53

You might as well try to outrun the wind or hold back a mountain-stream with a straw. I saw him, too, last night, and he was free!"

"I don't know what you mean," my brother replied in surprise, "but to us the discovery only increases our misery. Nobody would believe it at first, and even now Elizabeth will not be convinced in spite of all the evidence. Justine Moritz was so affectionate and kind to the family - who would guess that she could commit such a frightful crime?"

"Justine Moritz! Poor, poor girl, do they accuse her? Everyone should know she is wrongly accused. Surely nobody believes it, Ernest?"

"Nobody did believe at first, but several circumstances came out that almost forced us to believe. Her own behavior has seemed so confused, it has added to the facts and leaves little room for doubt. But, her trial is today, and you will hear everything."

Ernest told me that Justine had fallen ill on the same morning that William was murdered, and she had to stay in bed for several days. During this time, one of the servants happened to examine the clothes she was wearing on the night of the murder. In her pocket, the servant found the picture of my mother, which had supposedly tempted the murderer. The servant instantly showed the picture to one of the other servants, and they went to the magistrate without talking to the family. Justine was arrested based on their testimony. The poor girl seemed so confused, it only confirmed the suspicion.

It was a strange story, but it did not change my belief. I replied earnestly, "You are all mistaken. I know the murderer. Justine, poor, good Justine, is innocent."

At that moment, my father entered the room. His face reflected deep unhappiness, but he tried to welcome me cheerfully. We would have changed the subject after our first unhappy greeting if Ernest had not exclaimed, "Good God, Papa! Victor says he knows who murdered poor William."

"Unfortunately, we know as well," my father replied. "I would rather not know than discover such ingratitude and evil in somebody I valued so highly."

"My dear father, you are mistaken, Justine is innocent."

"If she is innocent, God forbid she should suffer as guilty. She will be tried today, and I hope, I sincerely hope, that she will be cleared."

His words calmed me. I was firmly convinced in my mind that Justine was innocent. No human being had committed this murder. I did not think circumstantial evidence against Justine could be strong enough to convict her. I could not tell my story publicly. People would consider it madness. Except for myself, the creator, who could believe in the existence of that monument to arrogance and rash ignorance which I had let loose on the world – unless they saw it themselves?

Elizabeth soon joined us. She had changed since I last saw her. Her loveliness had only increased with time. She had the same spirit and sincerity, but her expression revealed greater intelligence and maturity. She welcomed me with the greatest affection. "My dear cousin," she said, "your arrival fills me with hope. Maybe you will find some way to clear my poor innocent Justine. Alas! If she can be convicted of crime – who is safe? I believe in her innocence as surely as I believe in my own. Our misfortune is doubly hard for us. We have not simply lost this lovely, darling boy – but this poor girl will be torn away by a worse fate. I truly love Justine. If she is condemned, I will never be happy again. But she will not, I am sure she will not, and then I will be happy again, even after the sad death of my little William."

"She is innocent, my Elizabeth," I said, "and it shall be proved. Do not fear. We should remain cheerful and confident that she will be acquitted."

"You are so kind and generous! Everyone else believes in her guilt, and that has made me miserable. I know it is impossible that Justine is guilty, and it has made me feel hopeless and despair to see everyone else prejudiced against her." Elizabeth wept.

"Dearest niece," my father said, "dry your tears. If she is innocent, as you believe, we must trust in the justice of our laws. I will make sure the trail is fair."

Chapter 8

We passed a few sad hours until eleven o'clock when the trial began. My father and the rest of the family were required to attend as witnesses. I went with them to the court. During the whole wretched mockery of justice, I suffered living torture. The court would decide whether my curiosity and lawless action would cause the death of two of my fellow beings. One was a smiling child filled with innocence and joy. The other would be murdered in a far more horrible way. Justine had many good qualities which promised to bring her happiness, and now her happy life would be destroyed. She would go to her grave as a criminal, and I was the cause. I would have preferred confessing to the crime myself rather than watching Justine be accused, but I was not present when the murder was committed. My confession would be considered the raving of a madman, and it would not help clear Justine, who suffered through me.

Justine was dressed in mourning, and she appeared calm. Her expression was always appealing, and now her solemn feelings made her face appear exquisitely beautiful. She seemed confident in her innocence and did not tremble, even though thousands stared and insulted her. The crowd might have felt some sympathy when they considered her beauty, but all sympathy was obliterated by the horror of the murder. Justine seemed calm, but her calmness was controlled. Her previous confusion had been used as evidence against her, and Justine was determined to appear courageous. When she entered the court, she looked around and quickly found the place where we were sitting. Her eyes seemed to dim with tears when she saw us, but she quickly regained control of herself. Her expression of sorrowful affection seemed to proclaim her absolute innocence.

The trial began, and the prosecutor stated the charge. Several witnesses were called. Some strange facts combined to make the case against Justine. For people who did not know the truth about her innocence, as I did, the facts might seem suspicious. Justine was out the whole night of the murder, and toward morning a market-woman saw her near the place where the murdered child was found. The woman asked Justine what she was doing there, but she looked confused, and her response was difficult to understand. She returned to the house about eight o'clock. When she was asked where she had spent the night, Justine replied that she was looking for the child, and she asked earnestly whether the child had been found. When she was shown the body, she fell into hysterics and had to spend several days in bed. The picture which the servant had taken from her pocket was shown as evidence. When Elizabeth confirmed that it was the same picture which the child had begged to wear just one hour before he went missing, the court was filled with a murmur of horror and indignation.

Justine was called to speak in her own defense. Her expression had changed as the trial proceeded, and her face strongly conveyed surprise, horror, and misery. Sometimes she struggled to hold back her tears, but when she was asked to state her plea, she collected herself and replied in a voice that was shaky but clear.

"God knows," she said, "I am completely innocent. But, I do not expect my word alone to clear me. I will base my innocence on a plain and simple explanation of the facts that are brought against me. I hope that my good character will incline the judges to interpret my story favorably, if some of the facts seem doubtful or suspicious."

Justine stated that Elizabeth had given her permission to spend the evening with her aunt who lived at Chene, a village about one league away from Geneva, the night the murder took place. As she was returning, about nine o'clock, she met a man who asked if she had seen the lost child. She was alarmed by his news and spent several hours looking for William. Finding the city gates closed, she was forced to spend several hours of the night in a barn belonging to some people she knew. She remained awake and watchful during most of that time, but she fell asleep towards morning. She was wakened by the sound of footsteps. It was dawn, and she left her refuge, hoping again that she might find my brother. She did not know whether he might have approached the place where his body was found. It was not surprising that she seemed confused when she was questioned by the market-woman since she had scarcely slept that night, and she did not yet know what had happened to William. She could not explain how she came to have the picture.

"I know this one circumstance weighs fatally against me," she said, "but I have no explanation. I have tried to imagine who might have placed it in my pocket. As far as I know, I have no enemy on earth, and surely nobody would be wicked enough to destroy me on purpose. Did the murderer put it there? I don't know when he could have done it. If he did place it there, why would he steal the jewel and discard it so quickly?

I commit my case to the justice of my judges, but I am afraid to hope. I beg permission to bring forward a few witnesses to testify to my character. If their testimony does not counterbalance my supposed guilt, I will be condemned, though I would stake my soul on my complete innocence."

Several witnesses were called who had known Justine for many years. The witnesses spoke well of her, but they seemed timid and reluctant to come forward due to their fear and hatred of the crime. Elizabeth became violently agitated when she saw that Justine's excellent character would not help her. She requested permission to address the court.

"I am the cousin of the unhappy child who was murdered," she said. "You can say I was his sister because I have lived with his parents since long before he was born. It might seem indecent for me to come forward on this occasion. But, I must speak out when I see a fellow creature about to perish through the cowardice of her pretended friends. I must describe

59

what I know about Justine's character. I lived with Justine in the same household for five years in the past, and nearly two years now. She was consistently thoughtful and kind to others during that entire time. She nursed Madame Frankenstein, my aunt, during her final illness with the greatest affection and care. Afterward, she cared for her own mother during a long, difficult illness with patience that won the admiration of everyone who knew her. When Justine returned to my uncle's house, she was beloved by everybody in the family. She was very fond of the dead child, and she cared for him with motherly affection. For my own part, I do not hesitate to say, I am certain Justine is completely innocent in spite of the evidence against her. She had no reason to commit this crime. If Justine had wanted the picture, which seems to be the main point of evidence, I would have given it to her gladly – I respect and value her so highly."

A murmur of approval followed Elizabeth's simple and powerful statement. But, the approval was excited by her generous interference and not in favor of poor Justine. The public turned against Justine with renewed hatred, charging her with blackest ingratitude. Justine wept as Elizabeth spoke, but she did not respond. My own anguish was extreme, and I remained agitated during the entire trial. I knew Justine was innocent. I did not doubt for one minute that the demon had murdered my brother. Did he betray this innocent girl to shame and death, for hellish sport? I could not bear the horror of my position. The public comments, and the expressions of the judges, told me they had already condemned my unhappy victim. I rushed out of the court in agony. Justine did not suffer as much as I did, since she was sustained by her innocence, while my heart was torn by regret.

I spent the night in wretchedness. When I went to the court in the morning, my throat and lips were dry, and I did not dare to ask the fatal question. But, I was well-known there, and the officer guessed the reason I had come. He told me the ballots were cast, they were all black, and Justine was condemned.

I will not pretend to describe what I felt. I had experienced horror before, which I have tried to describe, but words cannot convey the heart-sickening despair I endured when I heard this news. The officer told me that Justine had already confessed her guilt. "We hardly needed her confession," he said, "the evidence was so glaring, but I am glad she has confessed. Judges never like to convict on circumstantial evidence even when it is decisive."

What could this strange news mean? Had my eyes deceived me? Was I really mad – as the whole world would declare if I revealed my suspicions? I hurried home, and Elizabeth eagerly demanded to know what had happened

"My cousin," I replied, "the judges have decided as you might have guessed. Judges always prefer that the innocent should suffer rather than one guilty person should escape. But, she has confessed."

It was a dreadful blow to Elizabeth who had firmly believed in Justine's innocence. "Alas!" she said, "how can I ever again trust human goodness? I loved and respected Justine as my sister. How could she smile with such innocence, only to betray us? She seemed incapable of deceit, and yet she has committed murder."

We soon received word that the poor victim had requested to see my cousin. My father did not want her to go, but he left the decision to her own feelings and judgment. "Yes," Elizabeth said, "I will go, even though she is guilty. I cannot go alone, Victor, you will come with me." The mere thought of this visit tortured me, yet I could not refuse. We entered the gloomy prison chamber and saw Justine sitting on some straw at the farther end. Her hands were shackled, and her head rested on her knees. She rose when she saw us, and when we were alone she threw herself down at Elizabeth's feet, weeping bitterly. My cousin wept as well.

"Oh, Justine!" she said, "You have taken away my last comfort. I believed you were innocent, and I was miserable, but not as miserable as I am now."

"Do you also believe I am so very, very wicked? Do you join with my enemies to crush me and condemn me as a murderer?" Justine's voice broke down in tears.

"Rise, my poor girl," Elizabeth said, "why do you kneel if you are innocent? I am not one of your enemies. I believed you were innocent, regardless of the evidence, until I heard that you had confessed. Be assured, Justine, nothing can shake my faith in you except your own confession."

"I did confess, but I confessed a lie. The God of heaven forgive me! Now the falsehood lies heavy on my heart. Ever since I was condemned, the priest has threatened and menaced until I almost believed I was the monster he said I was. He threatened me with excommunication and hellfire if I continued to be stubborn and did not confess. Dear lady, I had nobody to support me. Everyone looked upon me as a criminal doomed to shame and damnation. What could I do? I confessed to a lie, and now I am truly miserable."

Justine paused, weeping, and then she continued speaking. "I was horrified, my sweet lady, when I thought you would believe your Justine capable of such a crime. Your blessed aunt had always honored me so highly, and I know you loved me. Only the devil himself could have committed such a crime. Dear William! Dearest, blessed child! I will see you soon in heaven. Even as I face shame and death, it comforts me to think we will be happy."

"Oh, Justine! Forgive me for doubting you even for one moment. Why did you confess? But do not grieve, dear girl, do not fear. I will prove your innocence. I will melt the stony hearts of your enemies with my tears and prayers. You will not die!

You, my playmate, my companion, my sister, perish by hanging! No, no! I could never survive such a terrible misfortune."

Justine shook her head mournfully. "I am not afraid to die," she said, "that pain is over. God supports my weakness, and gives me courage to endure the worst. I leave a sad and bitter world. As long as you think of me, and remember me, as somebody who was condemned unjustly, I am resigned to my fate. Dear lady, we must submit to the will of heaven."

During this conversation, I had retreated to a corner of the prison room where I could conceal the horrid anguish that possessed me. Despair! Who dared to talk about despair? Justine would pass the awful boundary between life and death on the morrow. Even the poor victim did not feel such deep and bitter agony as I did. I ground my teeth and uttered a groan that came from my inmost soul. Justine was startled. When she saw who it was, she approached me and said, "Dear sir, you are very kind to visit me. I hope you do not believe I am guilty?"

I could not answer. "No, Justine," Elizabeth replied, "He is more convinced of your innocence than I was. Even when he heard about your confession, he did not believe it."

"I truly thank him. In these last moments, I am most grateful to those who think of me with kindness. The affection of others is sweet for someone as wretched as I am. Your kindness removes more than half my misfortune. I feel that I could die in peace now that you, dear lady, and your cousin have acknowledged my innocence."

In this way, the poor sufferer tried to comfort others and herself. I believe she gained the acceptance she desired. But, I was the true murderer. I felt the deathless worm alive in my heart which allowed no hope or comfort. Elizabeth wept, and she was unhappy, but she felt the misery of innocence. Her happiness might be clouded, but the brightness beneath could not be diminished. Anguish and despair had penetrated into the core of my heart. I carried a hell inside me that nothing could extinguish. We stayed with Justine for several hours, and Elizabeth tore herself away with great difficulty. "I wish I could die with you," she said, "I cannot live in this world of misery."

Justine pretended to be cheerful, and she repressed her bitter tears with great effort. She embraced Elizabeth and said in a voice half-choked with emotion, "Farewell, sweet lady, dearest Elizabeth, my beloved and only friend. May bountiful heaven bless you and preserve you. I pray that this is the last misfortune you will ever suffer! Live and be happy, and make others happy."

Justine died the next day. Elizabeth's heartfelt words did not change the judges' firm belief that the saintly sufferer was guilty. The judges ignored my passionate appeals. When I heard their cold answers and their harsh, unfeeling logic, the words I meant to say died away on my lips. I might convince them that I was a madman, but I could not change the sentence they imposed upon my wretched victim. She perished on the scaffold as a murderess.

I turned from my own tortured heart to consider the deep and voiceless grief of my Elizabeth. I was responsible for this as well. And my father's sorrow, and the desolation of this happy home, it was all the work of my accursed hands. You weep, unhappy ones, but these are not your last tears. Your funeral cries will be heard again. It would be happiness beyond hope if this destruction ended before all torment was silenced by the grave. I was torn by remorse, horror, and despair, and my soul seemed to gaze into the future. I looked around and saw the people I loved weeping over the graves of William and Justine, the first helpless victims of my sinister work.

∞∞∞∞∞∞∞∞∞∞∞∞∞∞∞∞∞∞∞∞∞∞∞∞

Chapter 9

Nothing is more painful to the human mind than the dead calm of inactivity and certainty that follows painful emotion and deprives the soul of both fear and hope. Justine was dead, she rested, and I was still alive. A weight of despair and remorse pressed on my heart, and nothing could remove it. I could not sleep, and I wandered like an evil spirit. I had committed acts that were horrible beyond description, and I was certain more horror would follow. Yet my heart overflowed with kindness and the desire to do good. I had started life with good intentions, and I had imagined the time when my discoveries might be useful to my fellow beings. Now my hope was blasted, and I was seized by remorse and guilt that carried me away to a hell of intense torture that words cannot describe.

My state of mind affected my health. It is possible that my health had never fully recovered from the shock of my illness. I avoided meeting people, and evidence of joy or contentment seemed like torture to me. Solitude was my only consolation - deep, dark, deathlike solitude.

My father was distressed by the change in my personality and habits. Guided by his own clear conscience and guiltless life, he tried to inspire me with the courage and strength to dispel the dark cloud that hung over me. "Do you think I do not suffer, Victor?" he said. "Nobody could love a child more than I loved your brother." His eyes filled with tears as he spoke. "But, it is our duty to the survivors not to increase their unhappiness by our own unrestrained grief. You have a duty to yourself as well, since excessive sorrow prevents improvement or enjoyment, and interferes with daily responsibilities which are necessary for life."

His advice was good, but it did not apply to my situation. I would be the first person to hide my grief and comfort my friends if bitter remorse and terror were not mixed with my other feelings. I could only give my father a despairing look and try to stay out of his way.

About this time, we moved to our small house at Belrive. The change was a relief to me. While we had lived in Geneva, the city gates were closed at ten o'clock every night, and I could never stay out on the lake after that time. Now I was free. I spent many hours on the lake after the family had gone to bed for the night. Sometimes I was carried by the wind, and sometimes I rowed to the middle of the lake and let the boat drift while I became lost in my own miserable thoughts. With the peaceful beauty surrounding me, it seemed that I was the only unquiet thing that wandered through the heavenly scene. I was often tempted to plunge into the silent lake and let the warm waters close over me and my troubles forever. But, I was restrained by the thought of Elizabeth, whose life was bound up with mine. She had suffered so much, and I loved her dearly. I thought about my father and surviving brother as well. I could not leave them exposed and unprotected from the fiend that I had let loose.

At these moments, I wept bitterly and wished that I could restore peace to my mind so that I could comfort my family. But, that was not possible. Remorse extinguished every hope. I could not undo the evil I had created, and I lived with constant fear that the monster would perpetrate some new wickedness. I had the vague feeling that things were not finished, and he would commit some truly terrible crime which would overshadow the past. I was forced to live in fear as long as the people I loved still remained. You cannot imagine how much I hated this fiend. When I thought about him, my eyes burned and I wanted to extinguish the life that I had thoughtlessly bestowed on him. When I considered his malice and crimes, my desire for revenge and my hatred exceeded all bounds. I would have traveled to the highest peak of the Andes, if I could have pushed him from the mountaintop. I wanted to see him again so that I could unleash my hatred upon him, and avenge the deaths of William and Justine.

Our house had become a house of mourning. My father's health was shaken by the horror of recent events. Elizabeth was depressed and unhappy, and she no longer enjoyed her ordinary occupations. She felt that enjoyment showed disrespect for the dead, and her tears and unhappiness were the only tribute she could give to the innocence which was blasted and destroyed. She was no longer the happy creature who had walked with me on the banks of the lake and talked with excitement about our future plans. Great sorrows come to detach us from life, and sorrow had quenched her youthful smiles.

"My dear cousin," she said, "when I think about the miserable death of Justine Moritz, I can no longer see the world the same way. Before, when I read about evil or heard stories about injustice, the evil seemed remote or far away. But now misery has come home, and men seem like monsters thirsting for each other's blood. Yet, I am surely being unfair. Everyone thought the poor girl was guilty. People thought she had murdered the son of her friends and benefactors for the sake of a few jewels. She had cared for the child since infancy, and seemed to love it as her own. I could not approve the death of any human being, but I should have thought she was unfit to live in society if she had really committed this crime. But, she was innocent. I feel certain she was innocent, and you feel the same way, which gives me support. Alas! Victor, when falsehood can look like truth, how can we trust in happiness? I feel like I am walking on top of a cliff, and crowds of people are trying to push me over the edge. William and Justine were killed, and the murderer has escaped. He is free to go where he likes, perhaps he is a respected person. But, I would not trade places with him, even if I had to die on the scaffold for the same crimes."

I felt the most extreme agony as I listened to her speak. I had not committed the acts, but I was the true cause of the murders. Elizabeth saw the anguished expression on my face, and she kindly took my hand. "My dearest friend, you must calm yourself," she said. "God knows how deeply these events have affected me. But, I am not as miserable as you are. Your look of despair and revenge makes me afraid. Victor, banish these dark passions. Remember that your family depends on you. Have we lost the power of making you happy? While we love, and we are true to each other, here in this beautiful country, we should enjoy every blessing of peace – what can bother us?"

I treasured Elizabeth more than any other gift life had given me. But, even her loving words could not chase away the fiend that lurked in my heart. As she spoke, I stepped closer to her, as if the destroyer was coming at that moment to take her from me.

My soul could not be saved from sorrow – not by friendship, or the beauty of earth or heaven, or even by the tenderness of love. I was trapped within a cloud which no happy influence could penetrate. I felt the way a wounded deer might feel when it has dragged itself into the bushes and gazes at the arrow that has pierced it.

Sometimes I could cope with the sullen despair that overwhelmed me. At other times, my state of mind became intolerable, and it seemed that exercise or change of scene was the only thing that could bring some relief from the whirlwind of passions within my soul. Driven by this mood, I suddenly left home one day and journeyed toward the Alpine valleys. Gazing upon the eternal magnificence of the mountain scenes, I tried to forget my temporary human sorrows. I wandered in the direction of the valley of Chamounix. I had visited this valley frequently during my boyhood. Six years had passed and turned me into a wreck, but nothing had changed about the wild, enduring scenes.

I traveled on horseback during the first part of the journey. Later I hired a mule since they are more sure-footed and less likely to be injured on the rugged roads. It was about the middle of August, and the weather was beautiful. Nearly two months had passed since Justine died. My spirit lightened as I approached the ravine of Arve. The immense mountain peaks that surrounded me on every side, the sound of the river raging among the rocks, the dashing of the waterfalls, these things spoke of a power that was Omnipotent. At that moment, I did not fear any being less than the Almighty who had created and ruled the elements. As I climbed higher, the valley appeared even more magnificent and astonishing. Ruined castles hung on the mountain peaks, and cottages were visible among the trees. The mighty Alps towered above everything, and the high mountains seemed to belong to another world where other beings lived.

I passed the bridge of Pelissier, where the ravine formed by the river opened before me. I began to climb the mountain that overhangs the ravine. Soon afterward, I entered the valley of Chamounix. This valley is more beautiful and sublime, though not as picturesque, as the valley of Servox which I had just passed through. The high, snowy mountains formed its boundaries, but I saw no more ruined castles or fertile fields. Immense glaciers flowed beside the road. I heard rumbling thunder and saw smoke from a falling avalanche. The supreme, magnificent Mont Blanc overlooked the valley.

A tingling, long-lost feeling of pleasure came to me during this journey. Some familiar turn in the road, or some new object that I recognized, reminded me of the lighthearted times of my boyhood. The winds seemed to whisper in a soothing way, and Mother Nature told me to weep no more. Then the influence of the scene faded – I found myself chained to grief again, and absorbed in my unhappy memories. I spurred my animal forward, trying to forget the world, my fears, and, most of all, myself. When I became more desperate, I dismounted and threw myself down on the grass, weighed down by horror and despair.

I finally arrived at the village of Chamounix. I was exhausted in body and mind after the extreme fatigue I had endured. For some time, I remained beside the window, watching the lighting flash weakly above Mont Blanc and listening to the rushing water of the Arve. The sounds worked as a lullaby for my overtired mind. Sleep came over me when I put my head down on the pillow, and I was grateful for the feeling of oblivion.

∞∞∞∞∞∞∞∞∞∞∞∞∞∞∞∞∞∞∞∞∞∞∞∞∞

Chapter 10

I spent the next day roaming through the valley. I stood beside the source of the Arveiron, where it rises from a glacier that flows slowly down from the peaks to barricade the valley. I saw the steep mountain-sides rising around me. The icy wall of the glacier hung over me, and a few shattered pine trees were scattered around. The silence of this glorious space was only broken by the thunder and crack of falling ice that echoed along the mountains. The magnificent scenes comforted me as much as anything could. The beauty did not remove my grief, but it soothed and diminished it. My mind was distracted from the thoughts that had consumed me for the past month. When I rested at night, my sleep was supported by the grand mountains I had seen during the day. They gathered around me - the unstained snowy mountain-tops, the shining peaks, the pine woods, the ragged bare ravine, the eagle flying amid the clouds - they all gathered around me and brought me peace.

What happened to this peace when I woke the next morning? My inspired feelings had vanished with sleep, and dark melancholy clouded every thought. Rain poured down in torrents, and thick mist hid the mountain-peaks. I was determined to penetrate the misty veil and see the mountains hiding behind the clouds. What was rain and storm to me? My mule was brought to the door, and I resolved to the climb to the summit of Montanvert. I remembered how I had felt when I first saw the tremendous flowing glacier. It had filled me with ecstasy which raised my soul from the ordinary world to regions of light and joy. The awful, majestic scenes of nature had always calmed my mind and helped me forget the worries of my life. I decided to go without a guide since I was familiar with the path, and the presence of another person would destroy the grand solitude.

The ascent is steep, but the path is gradual and winding, which allows you to climb up the steep mountainside. It is a

71

terrifically desolate scene. Traces of winter avalanche are visible in a thousand places. Trees are broken and strewn on the ground, some are entirely destroyed, and some are bent, leaning on the other trees or the jutting rocks. As you go higher, the path is intersected with ravines of snow, and rocks continuously roll down from above. Even one falling rock can be dangerous, since the slightest sound, even speaking loudly, can disturb the air enough to trigger an avalanche. The pines are not tall or luxuriant, but their darkness adds to the severity of the scene. I looked down upon the valley. Thick mist rose from the rivers below and curled around the mountain-tops. The peaks were hidden by clouds, and rain poured from the dark sky, contributing to the melancholy mood. Alas! Why do human beings boast of being superior to the animals? It only makes us more needy beings. If our needs were confined to hunger, thirst, and desire, we might be almost free. But, we are affected by every wind that blows, by every chance word that reminds us of some scene.

We sleep, and dreams poison sleep.
We rise, and one wandering thought poisons the day.
We feel, imagine, or reason, laugh or weep,
Embrace our sorrow, or cast sorrow away,
It makes no difference.
Our past might never be like our future.
Nothing is certain but change!

It was nearly noon when I arrived at the top of the mountain. For some time, I sat on the rock that overlooks the sea of ice. Mist covered the rock and the surrounding mountains. After a while, the breeze blew the clouds away, and I climbed down to the glacier. The surface was very uneven, rising and falling like waves, and criss-crossed by deep rifts. I spent almost two hours crossing the ice. The opposite mountain was a bare perpendicular rock. From the side where I now stood, Montanvert was directly in front of me, and Mont Blanc rose in awful majesty above it. I stayed in a recess of the rock, gazing at this wonderful, stupendous scene. The vast river of ice wound among the mountains, and the icy, glittering peaks shone in the sunlight over the clouds. My heart, which was sorrowful before, now swelled with something like joy. "Wandering spirits, allow me this small happiness," I exclaimed, "or take me with you away from the joys of life."

As I spoke, I saw the figure of a man some distance away, coming towards me at superhuman speed. He bounded over the rifts that I had carefully climbed over, and I noticed he seemed to be unusually tall. I started to feel faint, and my eyes grew dim, but the cold mountain breeze quickly revived me. The shape came closer, and I saw it was the wretch I had created. I trembled with rage and horror. I resolved to wait for his approach and then fight him to the death. He came closer, and I saw that his face expressed bitter anguish as well as disdain and malice. His unearthly ugliness made him almost too horrible for human eyes. But, I scarcely noticed how he looked. At first, I was speechless with rage, and when I recovered my voice, I could only express my hatred and contempt.

"Devil!" I exclaimed. "Do you dare approach me? You should fear my vengeance. Begone, vile insect! Or – stay – and I will trample you to dust! Oh! I wish I could restore the victims you murdered by erasing your existence."

"I expected this welcome," the devil replied. "All men hate those who are wretched. I am miserable beyond all living things, I know I must be hated! Yet you, my creator, detest and spurn me, your creature, even though we are bound by ties that only death can dissolve. You want to kill me. How dare you play with life this way? Do your duty towards me, and I will do my duty towards you and the rest of humankind. If you agree

73

with my conditions, I will leave you all at peace, but if you refuse, I will leave none of your friends alive."

"Disgusting monster! You are a fiend! The tortures of hell are not enough for your crimes. You reproach me with your creation, come I will extinguish the spark that I bestowed so carelessly."

My rage knew no bounds. I sprang towards him, propelled by all the hate that one being can feel towards another.

He easily eluded me. "Be calm," he said, "I beg you to listen before you say that you hate me. I have suffered enough, why do you want to increase my misery? Even though my life is nothing but pain, it has value to me, and I will defend it. Remember that you have made me stronger than yourself, I am taller than you, and my joints are more flexible. But, I will not be tempted to fight with you. I will consider you my lord and king, if you will do your part. You owe it to me. Oh, Frankenstein, do not be fair to everybody else and trample on me alone. You owe me your justice, and mercy and affection, more than you owe to others. I am your creature, but you have driven me from joy for no misdeed of my own. I see happiness everywhere, and I alone am excluded from it. I was kind and good, but misery had made me a fiend. Make me happy, and I will be good."

"Begone! I do not want to listen. There can be no bond between you and me, we are enemies. Begone, or let us fight and see who is stronger, and let one of us fall."

"How can I make you understand? What can I say to make you look kindly on me? I beg for your compassion and goodness. Believe me, Frankenstein, I was kind, and my soul glowed with humanity and love - but I am alone, miserably alone. You, my creator, hate me. What can I hope to receive from your fellow creatures who owe me nothing? They hate and detest me. The deserted mountains and the lonely glaciers are my refuge. I have wandered here for many days, since it is the only place people allow me to stay. I am the only one who is not afraid of the icy caves. I am pleased to see the bleak skies because they are kinder to me than your fellow beings. If humankind knew about my existence, they would do the same as you, and try to destroy me. Should I not hate the people who hate me? I owe nothing to my enemies. I am miserable, and they will share my misery. Yet, you have the power to make amends to me. You can save the people from evil, or you can make the evil greater, because thousands will be swallowed up by the whirlwind of rage along with you and your family. Show your compassion, and do not hate me. Listen to my story. When you have heard it, you can sympathize or abandon me as you think I deserve. But, hear me first. Even cruel human justice allows the guilty to speak in their own defense before they are condemned. Listen to me, Frankenstein. You accuse me of murder, yet you would destroy your own creature with a clear conscience. Praise the justice of human beings! I do not ask you to spare me, I simply ask you to listen and then, if you can, destroy the work of your own hands."

"Why do you make me recall events that are horrible beyond remembering?" I replied. "Hated devil, it was a cursed day when you first saw light. The hands that formed you were cursed, though they were my own. You have made me more wretched than I can say. You have left me with no power to consider whether I am fair to you or not. Begone! Remove your hated self from my sight."

"Let me help you, my creator," he said and put his hands in front of my eyes. "I can remove myself from your sight, and you can still listen and grant me your compassion." I flung his hands away from me. "By the goodness that you once possessed, I demand that you listen to me," he continued. "Hear my story. It is long and strange, and you cannot withstand the temperature here. Come to the hut upon the mountain. The sun is still high in the sky, you can hear my story before the day is over and make your decision. You will decide if I stay away from humankind forever and live a harmless life – or become the destroyer of your fellow creatures and the cause of your own speedy ruin."

As he spoke, he led the way across the ice, and I followed. My heart was full, and I did not answer him. But, as I walked, I considered the various arguments he had presented, and decided I should at least listen to his story. I was moved by both curiosity and compassion. I had believed him to be the murderer of my brother, and I was eager to hear the truth. For the first time, I began to consider what the duties of a creator to his creature might be. I felt that I should try to make him happy before I complained about his wickedness. I agreed with his demand, and we crossed the ice and climbed the rock in front of us. It was cold, and the rain began to fall. When we entered the hut, the fiend seemed joyful, while I felt heavy and depressed. But, I had agreed to listen, and I seated myself beside the fire, which my odious companion had lighted. He began his story.

Chapter 11

"It is hard for me to remember very much about the first part of my life. Everything from that time seems hazy and confused. I was overwhelmed by different sensations, and I saw, heard, felt, and smelled all at once. It was a long time before I learned to distinguish between the different senses. Gradually, I perceived the daylight shining brightly, and I was forced to close my eyes. When I opened my eyes, I saw the light was still there. Before, dark figures had surrounded me, now I found that I could walk forward without stumbling over obstacles. The light bothered me more and more, and walking in the heat made me tired. I looked for a place where I could rest in the shade. I found myself in the forest near Ingolstadt, and I lay down by the side of a brook, resting from my fatigue, until hunger and thirst began to torment me and roused me from my dormant state. I ate some berries which I found hanging on the trees or lying on the ground. I drank some water from the brook, and then I fell asleep.

It was dark when I woke up. I felt cold, and instinctively I felt frightened at finding myself alone. Before I left your apartment, I had covered myself with some clothes, but they were not enough to protect me from the cold night. I was a poor, helpless, miserable wretch. I knew nothing, and I could understand nothing, but I felt pain on all sides, and I sat down and wept.

Gentle light filled the sky, and I began to feel better. I looked up and saw a radiant form rising from the trees. It was the moon, and I gazed at it with wonder. It moved slowly, but it lighted my path, and I set out to search for berries. Under one of the trees, I found a huge cloak. I was still cold, and I sat down and covered myself with the cloak. My mind was confused, and I could not think clearly. I felt light, and hunger, and thirst, and darkness. I was surrounded by sounds and smells. The only object I could perceive clearly was the moon, and I looked at it with pleasure.

Several days and nights passed, and the moon had waned, when I began to distinguish my different senses from each other. Gradually, I could see the stream that gave me water, and the trees that gave me shade. I was delighted when I first discovered that a pleasant sound I had noticed earlier came from small creatures that flew through the air. I began to observe the forest around me in greater detail. Sometimes, I tried to imitate the pleasant songs of the birds, but I could not. Sometimes I tried to express my feeling in my own way, but the sounds I made frightened me into silence again.

I remained in the forest as the moon disappeared from the sky, and then appeared again in smaller form. By this time, my senses had become very sharp, and my mind formed new ideas every day. My eyes became accustomed to the daylight. I could distinguish plants from insects, and gradually I could distinguish the different plants from each other. I learned that the sparrow made harsh noises, while the thrush and the blackbird made sweet music.

One day, when I was feeling particularly cold, I found a fire which some wandering beggars had left lighted. I was overcome by delight at the warmth. In my joy, I put my hand into the live embers and quickly pulled it out again with a cry of pain. How strange that the same fire could cause such opposite sensations! I examined the materials of the fire, and I was pleased to find it was made of wood. I quickly collected some branches, but they were wet and they would not light. I was disappointed and sat watching the fire burn. The wet wood, which I placed near the fire, dried from the heat and caught fire itself. I realized the cause and became busy collecting wood so that I could dry it and have a plentiful supply of fire. When night came, I feared that my fire would be extinguished while I slept. I covered it carefully with dry wood and leaves, and put wet branches over it, and then I spread my cloak on the ground and fell asleep.

When I woke in the morning, the first thing I did was visit the fire. I uncovered it, and the gentle breeze quickly fanned the flame. I observed this and made a fan from branches which I could use to rouse the embers when they died down. When night came again, I discovered that the fire gave both light and heat. It was useful for my food as well. The beggars had left the remains of their food scattered around, and I found that their cooked food tasted better than the berries I had gathered from the trees. I tried to cook my food in the same way, putting it onto the live embers. I found that cooking spoiled the berries, but the nuts and roots were much improved.

As time passed, food became scarce, and I often spent the whole day searching for a few acorns to satisfy my hunger. I decided to move to a new place where food might be more plentiful. I was extremely sorry to leave the fire behind, because I did not know how to recreate it. I spent several hours thinking about this difficulty, but I was forced to give up, and finally wrapped myself in my cloak and set off into the woods towards the setting sun. I spent three days walking through the woods and finally reached open country. Snow had fallen the night before, and the white fields appeared bleak. My feet were chilled by the cold, damp stuff that covered the ground.

It was about seven o'clock in the morning, and I longed to find food and shelter. After some time, I noticed a small hut built on rising ground, perhaps for the use of a shepherd. I had never seen a hut before, and I examined it carefully from the outside. Finding the door open, I went inside. An old man was sitting near the fire preparing his breakfast. Hearing the noise, he turned, and when he saw me he shrieked loudly and ran away across the fields, faster than his withered form seemed capable of moving. His appearance and his flight surprised me. But, I was enchanted by the hut. Snow and rain could not penetrate here, the ground was dry, and it seemed like a heavenly refuge to me after my sufferings. I greedily devoured the remains of the shepherd's breakfast, which consisted of bread, cheese, milk, and wine. I did not like the wine. Overcome by fatigue, I lay down in the straw and fell asleep.

It was noon when I woke, and I decided to continue my journey, drawn by the warmth of the sun shining on the white ground. I put the remains of the peasant's breakfast into a wallet that I found and traveled across the fields for several hours. At sunset, I came to a village. It seemed like a miraculous place. I admired the huts, the neat cottages, and the stately houses. The vegetables in the gardens and the milk and cheese placed at the windows awakened my appetite. I entered one of the houses, but as soon as I stepped inside, the children shrieked, and one of the women fainted. The whole village was roused. Some people fled, and some attacked me. Bruised by stones and other flying objects, I escaped to the open country and fearfully took refuge in a low hovel, which seemed bare and wretched compared to the large houses in the village. The hovel stood close beside a neat, pleasant cottage but I did not dare approach the cottage after my recent experience. My refuge was built of wood, but it was so low that I could barely sit upright inside it. The floor was earth, and wind entered through cracks in the walls, but it gave me protection from the snow and rain.

I was happy to have found a shelter, no matter how miserable, from the winter weather and the barbarity of humans. As soon as morning came, I crept outside and looked at the cottage to see if I might stay in the place I had found. The hovel was located against the back of the cottage, and it had a pigsty and a pool of clear water on two sides. One side was open, and I had entered that way, but now I covered every crevice with stones and wood, though I could still move them to pass through. The only light came through the pigsty, but it was enough for me.

I covered the floor of my dwelling with clean straw, and then I retreated. I saw the figure of a man in the distance and I wanted to stay hidden, remembering how people had treated me the night before. Before retreating, I took a loaf of coarse bread and a cup, so that I could drink more easily from the clear pool beside the hovel. The floor was higher than the surrounding ground, and it stayed perfectly dry, and it was tolerably warm from the cottage-chimney nearby.

I decided to stay in this hovel until something should happen to change my circumstances. It seemed like a paradise compared to my former existence in the cold, wet forest. I finished my breakfast with pleasure, and I was about to get some water, when I looked out and saw a young woman with a pail in her hand passing in front of the hovel. She had a gentle demeanor, unlike most of the farmhouse servants and cottagers I met later. She was poorly dressed, wearing a coarse blue petticoat and a linen jacket. Her fair hair was plainly braided. She looked patient yet sad. She moved beyond my sight, and then returned after fifteen minutes carrying the pail which was now partly filled with milk. As she walked along, carrying her burden with some difficulty, she was met by a young man who had an unhappy expression. He said something, and then took the pail from her hand and carried it into the cottage himself. She followed him, and they disappeared from sight. After a little while, I saw the young man come out of the cottage carrying some tools in his hand. He crossed the field behind the cottage, and then the girl became busy in the house and the yard.

When I examined further, I found that one of the cottage windows formed part of the wall of my hovel. The window-panes were covered with wood, but there was a small hole in one place which allowed me to see inside. I saw a small room, white-washed and clean, but nearly bare of furniture. An old man sat in one corner near a small fire. He leaned his head on his hands in a despondent attitude. The girl was moving things around inside the cottage. She took something out of a drawer, which kept her hands busy, and sat down beside the old man. He picked up an instrument and began to play, producing sounds sweeter than the thrush or the nightingale. It was a lovely sight, even to me who had never seen beauty before. The silver hair and kind face of the old cottager awakened my respect, and the gentle manners of the girl inclined me to feel love. He played a sweet, mournful tune, and I saw the girl wiping her eyes. The old man did not seem to notice, until she sobbed out loud, and then he made a few sounds, and the girl left her work and knelt at his feet. He raised her, and smiled with such affection and kindness, that I was overpowered by sensations I had never felt before from hunger or cold, warmth or food. The feelings gave me both pain and pleasure, and I withdrew from the window, unable to bear the emotions.

Soon afterward, the young man returned, carrying a load of wood on his shoulders. The girl met him at the door and helped him put down the wood. She took some of the wood into the cottage and placed it on the fire. The young man took the girl aside and showed her a large loaf of bread and piece of cheese. The girl seemed pleased, and she went into the garden to gather some roots and plants, which she placed into water, and then put on the fire. She continued her work inside the cottage, and the young man went outside and appeared busy digging and pulling roots. After he had worked for one hour, the young woman joined him, and they went into the cottage together.

The old man had appeared thoughtful while he was alone, but he seemed more cheerful when his companions entered the room. They sat down to eat and quickly finished the meal. The young woman became busy again moving things around the cottage. The old man walked back and forth in front of the cottage in the sunshine, leaning on the young man's arm. Nothing could be more beautiful than the contrast between these two excellent creatures. The older man had silver hair, and his face glowed with kindness and love. The younger man was slight and graceful with attractive features, but his face and eyes expressed sadness and despair. The old man went back into the cottage after a few minutes, and the young man took some different tools and walked away across the fields.

Night fell quickly, and I was astonished to see that the cottagers had a way to make the light last longer by using candles. I was pleased that sunset did not end the pleasure I felt in watching my human neighbors. During the evening, the young man and the girl were busy with different occupations. The old man again played the instrument that had enchanted me in the morning with its divine sounds. When he had finished, the young man began to produce monotonous sounds, which did not seem like the music of the old man's instrument or the songs of birds. Later I learned that he was reading aloud, but at the time I knew nothing about books or letters.

After a short time, the family extinguished their lights and retired to rest.

∞∞∞∞∞∞∞∞∞∞∞∞∞∞∞∞∞∞∞∞∞

Chapter 12

I lay down on my straw, but I could not sleep. I thought about the happenings of the day. I was mainly struck by the gentle manners of the people. I longed to join them but I did not dare, remembering how the barbarous villagers had treated me. I decided that I would stay hidden in my place for the moment and try to learn more about the people's lives.

The cottagers rose before sunrise the next morning. The young woman prepared the food, and the young man left the cottage after the first meal.

The routine on this day was the same as the day before. The young man was constantly busy outdoors, while the young woman worked inside the cottage. I soon realized the old man was blind, and he spent his time playing on the instrument or thinking. The two young people showed the greatest love and respect for the old man. Every duty or action they performed for him was done with affection and gentleness, and he rewarded them with his kind smiles.

They were not entirely happy. The young man and woman often talked by themselves and seemed to weep. I saw no cause for their unhappiness, but it touched me deeply. If such lovely creatures could be miserable, it seemed less strange that a lonely, imperfect being like me should be wretched. They lived in a delightful house (it seemed to me) with a fire to warm them when they were cold. They ate delicious food when they were hungry and wore excellent clothes. Even more important, they enjoyed each other's company and speech, exchanging looks of affection and kindness every day. What did their tears mean? Did they really express pain? I could not answer these questions, but time and constant observation explained many things that seemed mysterious at first.

Considerable time passed before I realized one of the causes of distress for this family. It was poverty, and they suffered from poverty to a distressing degree. Their food consisted entirely of vegetables from their garden, and the milk of one cow. The cow gave little milk during the winter when its masters could barely give it enough food to stay alive. I believe the two younger cottagers frequently suffered from hunger, because several times I saw them put food in front of the old man when they had nothing themselves.

I was greatly moved by the kindness they showed. I had grown accustomed to stealing part of their store for myself during the night. When I found this caused pain for the cottagers, I stopped taking their food and satisfied myself with berries, roots, and nuts which I found in the nearby woods.

I discovered another way to help them as well. I noticed that the young man spent a large part of each day gathering wood for the family fire. During the night, I took his tools, which I quickly learned to use, and gathered enough firewood to last for several days.

I remember the first time I did this, the young woman opened the door in the morning, and she was astonished to see the large pile of wood outside. She spoke some words in a loud voice. The young man joined her, and he was surprised as well. I was pleased to see that he did not go into the forest that day, but spent the day repairing the cottage and working in the garden.

Gradually, I discovered something that was even more important. I learned that these people had a way of communicating their experiences and feelings to each other by making sounds. I observed that the words they spoke elicited pleasure or pain, smiles or sadness, from their listeners. I desperately wanted to learn this godlike science, but my attempts were unsuccessful. They spoke quickly, and their words did not seem to refer to any objects that I could see. I could find no clue to unravel the mystery of their speech. I kept trying, and after I had lived in my hovel for several months, I did learn the names for the most common subjects of conversation such as 'fire,' 'milk,' 'bread,' and 'wood.' I learned the names of the cottagers as well. The young man and woman had several names, but the old man had just one name, which was 'father.' The young woman was called 'Agatha' or 'sister.' The young man was 'Felix,' 'brother,' or 'son.' I cannot describe how delighted I felt when I first learned to say these words. I learned several other words as well, including 'good,' 'dearest,' and 'unhappy,' though I did not understand them.

I spent the winter in this way. The gentle manners and beauty of the cottagers made me feel attached to them. When they were unhappy, I felt depressed, and when they were joyful, I rejoiced. I saw few human beings besides these people. When other people did enter the cottage, their rude, harsh manners only confirmed my opinion that my friends were superior. I saw that the old man often encouraged his children to cast off their sadness. He would talk to them cheerfully with such an expression of goodness that he encouraged even me. Agatha would listen respectfully, trying to wipe away her tears without his noticing. I observed that her expression and tone were generally more cheerful after listening to her father. This was not true for Felix. He was always the saddest member of the group. Even to my inexperienced eyes, it seemed that he had suffered more than the rest of his family. Although his expression was more sorrowful, his voice was more cheerful than his sister, especially when he spoke to his father.

I could describe many small actions that revealed the character of these kindly cottagers. Living in the midst of poverty, Felix brought his sister the first little white flower than peeped out from beneath the snow. Early in the morning, before she woke, he cleared away the snow that blocked her path to the milk-house. He drew water from the well, and brought wood from the outhouse, where he was always astonished to find that some invisible hand had replenished the supply. I believe that he sometimes worked for a neighboring farmer during the day, because he often went out and did not return until dinner, yet did not bring home any wood. At other times, he worked in the garden, but there was little to do in the garden during the winter, and then he read to the old man and Agatha.

Reading had puzzled me extremely at first. Slowly, I discovered that Felix made many of the same sounds while reading as he did while speaking. I guessed that he was able to understand signs for speech that were written on the paper. I desperately wished that I could understand as well, but how could I read when I did not even speak? My ability to say words gradually improved, though not enough for me have a conversation. I put all my effort into learning words. I wanted to make myself known to the cottagers, but I realized that I should not try to meet them until I could speak more of their language. Perhaps they would overlook my deformed figure if I could speak to them. From constantly watching them, I realized how different I appeared.

I had admired the perfect form of my cottagers – their grace, and beauty, and delicate features. How terrified I felt when I saw my own reflection in a pool of water! At first, I was startled, and could not believe that the reflection was really me. When I became fully convinced that I really was the monster than I am, I was filled with shame and despair. Alas! I did not yet understand the fatal consequences of my miserable deformity.

The days grew longer, the sunshine became warmer, and the snow vanished. I saw the bare trees and the black earth. Felix had more employment, and the family had enough to eat. Their food was coarse, but it was wholesome and plentiful. Several new plants sprang up in the garden and added to their diet. The family grew more comfortable as the season advanced.

Every day at noon, when it did not rain, the old man walked in front of the house, learning on his son's arm. It rained often, but the high wind quickly dried the earth. The weather became much more pleasant than before.

The pattern of my life in the hovel did not change. During the mornings, I observed the actions of the cottagers. When they became busy with tasks, I slept, and then I resumed 6atching my friends. After they had gone to bed, I went into the forest, if there was any moon or starlight, and collected my own food and wood for the cottage. When I returned, I cleared away snow from the path and did some of the tasks I had seen Felix do. I learned later that my secret work astonished them, and I heard them say 'good spirit' and 'wonderful' though I did not understand the meaning of the words.

I began to think more clearly, and I longed to understand the feelings and intentions of these lovely creatures. I was curious to know why Felix seemed so miserable, and Agatha seemed sad. I foolishly imagined that I might be able to help these deserving people. When I slept, or left the cottage, I recalled the forms of the respectable, blind father, the gentle Agatha, and the excellent Felix. I looked up to them as superior beings who would determine my future destiny. I imagined a thousand different ways that I might present myself to them, and how they would respond. I imagined they would be disgusted, but I would win their acceptance, and later their love, with my gentle manners and words.

I was excited by this thought, and renewed my efforts to learn language. Their voices sounded like soft music compared with mine, but I could easily pronounce the few words I knew. My voice might resemble the braying of a donkey or the barking of a lap-dog, but surely if the donkey was affectionate and gentle, he deserved better treatment than blows and insults.

The mild rain showers and pleasant warmth of spring changed the appearance of everything. Men emerged from their hiding places and became active cultivating the land. The birds sounded more cheerful, and the leaves began to bud on the trees.

Happy, happy earth! It had seemed bleak, damp, and unhealthy such a short time before. Now it had become a habitation fit for the gods. The enchanting appearance of nature lifted my spirits. The past was blotted from my memory, I felt content with the present, and I looked forward to the future with hope and joy.

Chapter 13

Now I will move ahead to the more interesting part of my story. I will describe my feelings about events that transformed me from what I was into what I have become.

Spring advanced quickly with fine weather and cloudless skies. It surprised me to see the gloomy, barren land covered with the most beautiful flowers and greenery. My senses were refreshed by a thousand delightful scents and a thousand beautiful sights.

My cottagers rested periodically from their labors. When they were resting one day, the old man was playing on his guitar, and the children were listening to him. Felix seemed unusually melancholy. When he sighed, I saw his father pause in his music and ask him what was wrong. Felix answered him cheerfully, and the old man was about to start playing again, when somebody tapped on the door.

It was a lady on horseback, and she was accompanied by a country-man as a guide. The lady was wearing a dark suit and covered with a thick black veil. Agatha asked her a question, and she responded by speaking the name of Felix in a sweet voice. Her voice was musical, but it sounded different from my friends. Hearing his name, Felix quickly approached the lady. She threw up her veil, revealing her angelic beauty. She had shining raven-black hair, curiously braided, and her dark eyes were gentle and bright. She had regular features, and her fair complexion was tinged with a lovely pink.

Felix seemed overcome with delight when he saw her. The sorrow disappeared instantly from his face, and it was replaced by ecstatic joy. I could hardly believe he was capable of such a joyful expression. His eyes sparkled, and his cheeks flushed with pleasure. At that moment, I thought he looked as beautiful as the stranger. She seemed moved by different feelings. She wiped a few tears from her lovely eyes as she held out her hand to Felix. He kissed her hand with rapture, and I thought he called her his sweet Arabian. She smiled, though she did not seem to understand him. He helped her dismount from the horse, dismissed her guide, and led her into the cottage. Some conversation took place between Felix and his father. The young stranger knelt down at the old man's feet, and she would have kissed his hand, but he raised her and embraced her affectionately.

While the stranger spoke in her own language, I soon realized that she did not understand the cottagers, and they did not understand her. They communicated using gestures that I did not understand, but I saw that she brought happiness to the cottage. Her presence diffused their sorrow as the sun diffuses the morning mist. Felix seemed especially happy, and he welcomed his Arabian with smiles of delight. Gentle Agatha kissed the lovely stranger's hands. She pointed to her brother, and her gestures seemed to mean he had been unhappy until the stranger came. Some hours passed, and their faces expressed joy that I did not understand. I observed that the stranger frequently attempted to repeat the sounds they made, in order to learn their language. I decided that I would watch and learn as well. The stranger learned about twenty words during the first lesson. Most were words I had learned before, but I learned some words that were new.

When night came, Agatha and the Arabian retired early. Before they left, Felix kissed the stranger's hand and said, 'Good night, sweet Safie.' He stayed awake much longer, talking with his father. Hearing her name repeated frequently, I guessed that they were talking about their lovely guest. I wished that I could understand them, and I did my best to comprehend their words, but I found it impossible.

The next morning, Felix went out to work. When Agatha had finished her usual tasks, the Arabian sat down near the old man's feet. She took his guitar and played some music that was so entrancingly beautiful, my eyes filled with tears of sorrow and delight. She sang, and the rich cadence of her voice flowed and swelled like the nightingale of the woods.

When she had finished, she gave the guitar to Agatha, who refused at first before taking it. Agatha played a simple song, and her sweet voice accompanied the music, but it was different from the wondrous music of the stranger. The old man seemed enraptured, and he said some words that Agatha tried to explain to Safie. The old man wanted to express that she had given him the greatest delight with her music.

The days passed as peacefully as before with the difference that joy had replaced the sadness on my friends' faces. Safie was always gay and happy. She and I improved rapidly in knowledge of language. By the end of two months, I understood most of the family's speech.

During this time, greenery covered the black ground, and the green banks were covered with countless flowers that were sweet to the nose and the eyes. The sun grew warmer, the nights were clear and mild, and the stars shone radiantly over the moonlit woods. I greatly enjoyed my nightly rambles, even though my outings were shortened by the late setting and early rising of the sun. I never went out during the day, afraid the people would attack me as they had in the first village I had entered.

I continued my efforts to learn language, and I may boast that I learned more quickly than the Arabian, who understood little and spoke in broken accents. I could understand and imitate almost every world that was spoken.

While I improved in speech, I also learned how to read by listening to the lessons taught to the stranger. Reading opened a wide field of wonder and delight for me.

The book which Felix used to teach Safie was Volney's *Ruins of Empire.* I would not have understood the meaning of this book if Felix had not explained it in detail as he read. He said he had chosen the book because the style of writing resembled the Eastern authors. This book taught me about the history of the various empires that exist in the world. I learned about the manners, governments, and religions of the different countries of the world. I heard about the laziness of the Asians, the tremendous genius and mental activity of the Greeks, the wonderful virtue and wars of the early Romans, their later decline and the downfall of their mighty empire, about chivalry, Christianity, and kings. I heard about the discovery of the American hemisphere and wept with Safie over the terrible fate of its original inhabitants.

This wonderful narrative inspired me with strange feelings. Was it possible for humans to be so powerful, virtuous, and magnificent, and so vicious and low? Sometimes, humans seemed to embody the principle of evil, and other times they seemed noble and godlike. Being great and virtuous seemed to be the highest honor that a sensitive person could achieve. Many people throughout history had been vicious and low. They seemed degraded, lower than the blind mole or the harmless worm. For a long time, I could not understand how one man could kill his fellow man, or why laws and governments should exist. I stopped wondering when I heard the details of vice and bloodshed and turned away with disgust and loathing.

Every conversation among the cottagers now taught me new things. By listening to Felix teach the Arabian, I learned about the strange systems of human society. I learned about the division of property, about immense wealth and squalid poverty, about rank, descent, and noble blood.

The words made me think about myself. I learned that what people valued most was high, unsullied descent combined with wealth. A man might be respected if he had either descent or wealth, but without either one he was considered a vagabond or slave. Except in rare cases, he was doomed to waste his life working to profit the chosen few! What was I? I knew nothing about my creation or my creator, but I knew that I had no money, no friends, no property of any kind. Moreover, I had a hideously deformed and loathsome appearance. I seemed to be a different kind of being, taller and quicker than humans. I could withstand greater extremes of heat and cold, and survive on a coarser diet. When I looked around, I saw nobody like me. People had run from me and disowned me. Was I a monster, then, some kind of stain upon the earth?

My thoughts were agonizing. I tried to push the thoughts away, but my sorrow only increased as I learned more. If only I had remained in my native forest forever, and knew nothing beyond the sensations of hunger, thirst, and heat!

Knowledge is a strange thing! It clings to the mind the way moss clings to a rock once it has taken hold. Sometimes I wanted to rid myself of all thought and feeling, but I learned there was only one way to stop feeling pain – and that was death. I feared death, though I did not understand it. I admired my cottagers for their virtuous character and gentle manners, but I was shut out from their company. My secret interaction with them did not satisfy me, it only made me want their friendship more. Agatha's gentle words, and the charming smiles of the

94

Arabian, were not for me. The mild encouragement of the old man, and the lively conversation of Felix was not for me

I learned other lessons as well that affected me even more deeply. I heard about the difference between the sexes, and the birth and growth of children. I learned that fathers were delighted by the smiles of their infants and the lively play of older children; and, mothers devoted all their life and care to their precious responsibility. Young people grew and gained knowledge about the world.   I learned about brothers and sisters and all the different relationships that connected human beings to each other.

Where were my friends and relatives? No father had watched over my infant days, no mother had blessed me with smiles and caresses – or, if they had, I did not remember. My past life seemed like a blank, vacant space which had left no trace. I had been the same size and height for as long as I could remember. I had never yet seen a being who looked like me, or tried to interact with me in any way. What was I? I asked myself the question over and over, and I could only groan in reply.

I will soon explain the outcome of my self-reflection, but first I will continue the story of the cottagers, which inspired me with delight, wonder, and indignation. I foolishly liked to call them my protectors, and my love for them grew.

∞∞∞∞∞∞∞∞∞∞∞∞∞∞∞∞∞∞∞

Chapter 14

Some time passed before I learned the full history of my friends. I had experienced so little, I was easily impressed by their interesting, wonderful circumstances.

The old man's name was De Lacey. He came from a good family in France, where he had lived comfortably for many years. He was respected by his superiors and beloved by his equals. His son was raised to serve his country, and Agatha was considered a high-ranking lady. A few months before I arrived, they had lived in a large, luxurious city called Paris. Surrounded by friends, they had every enjoyment that virtue, intellect, and taste, combined with moderate fortune, could afford them.

Safie's father was the cause of their ruin. He was a Turkish merchant, who had lived in Paris for many years. For some reason that I did not understand, he lost favor with the government. He was seized and put into prison on the very same day that Safie arrived from Constantinople to join him. He was tried and condemned to death. His sentence was flagrantly unfair, and all of Paris was indignant on his behalf. People felt that the judgment against him was based on his religion and wealth, and not on his alleged crime.

Felix happened to be present at the trial. He could not control his horror and indignation when he heard the decision of the court. In that moment, he made a solemn vow to rescue the merchant, and he began to think of a plan. First, he tried to gain entrance to the prison. After many unsuccessful attempts, he found that the grated window lighting the dungeon was unguarded. Loaded with chains, the unlucky Mohammedan waited in despair for the execution of the cruel sentence. Felix came to the window at night, and told the prisoner he had come to help. The Turk was delighted and amazed, and he tried to motivate his rescuer by promising to reward him with wealth.

Felix rejected his offers with contempt. But, he was forced to admit that the captive did have one treasure that might reward his efforts. Safie was allowed to visit her father, and through her gestures she expressed her lively gratitude to Felix.

The Turk soon noticed that his daughter had made a deep impression on Felix's heart. He tried to make certain that Felix would help him by promising to give Felix his daughter's hand in marriage as soon as he was taken to a place of safety. Felix was too refined to accept this offer, but he looked forward to the possibility of the marriage as the fulfillment of his happiness.

During the following days, Felix went forward with preparations for the merchant's escape, and he was inspired by several letters that he received from the lovely girl. She found a way to express her thoughts in language that her lover could understand with the help of her father's old servant who understood French. She thanked Felix in the most passionate terms for his services to her father. At the same time, she lamented her own fate.

I have copies of these letters. While I stayed in the hovel, I obtained tools for writing, and Felix and Agatha often looked at the letters. I will give you the letters before I leave, but for now I will summarize what they said, since the sun is already declining, and the afternoon is growing late. The letters will prove the truth of my story.

Safie wrote that her mother was a Christian Arab who was seized and enslaved by the Turks. Safie's father was charmed by her beauty, and he had married her. Safie's mother was born in freedom, and she spurned her life of bondage. The young girl spoke about her mother in terms of the highest praise. Safie's mother instructed her daughter in her own religion. She encouraged Safie to develop her intellect and independent spirit in a way that was forbidden for Muhammadan women. Her mother had died, but her lessons were impressed on Safie's mind. She felt sick at the prospect of returning to Asia and being confined within the walls of a harem. She would be forced to occupy herself with childish amusements that were not suited to her character, especially now that she had grown accustomed to grand ideas and the pursuit of virtue. She was captivated by the thought of marrying a Christian and staying in a country where women were allowed to participate in society.

The date was set for the Turk's execution, but he escaped from the prison the night before. By the next morning he was many leagues away from Paris. Felix had obtained passports for his father, sister, and himself. He had previously shared his plan with his father. His father had assisted in the deception by leaving his house under the pretext of taking a journey, and coming to stay in Paris with his daughter.

Felix guided the fugitives through France to Lyons, and across Mont Cenis to Leghorn, where the merchant waited for a favorable opportunity to travel into Turkey.

Safie decided to stay with her father until he departed, and he promised that she should be married to the man who had rescued him. Felix stayed with them, waiting for the marriage to take place. During that time, he enjoyed the company and the simple, tender affection of the Arabian. They spoke to each other using an interpreter, and sometimes using the language of looks, and Safie sang the divine songs of her native country.

The Turk encouraged the hopes of the young lovers, and he allowed them to spend time together, even though he had secretly made other plans. He hated the idea that his daughter should marry a Christian, but he was afraid Felix would be angry if he seemed to change his mind. He still depended on Felix not to betray him to the authorities in Italy where they were living. He planned to prolong the deceit for as long as possible, and then take his daughter with him when he left. The news from Paris made his plan easier.

The government in Paris was enraged by the Turk's escape. The officials spared no effort to find and punish his rescuer. Felix's plot was quickly discovered, and De Lacey and Agatha were thrown into prison. Felix heard the news and woke from his dream of pleasure. His blind, elderly father and his gentle sister were held in a foul dungeon, while he enjoyed freedom and the company of the woman he loved. This thought tortured him. Felix left the lovely Arabian and hurried to Paris where he surrendered to the vengeance of the law. He hoped to free De Lacey and Agatha through this action. The Turk agreed to leave Safie at a convent in Leghorn if he found the opportunity to escape before Felix could return to Italy.

Felix did not succeed in freeing his family. They remained confined in jail for five months. When the trial took place, they were deprived of their fortune and permanently exiled from their native country.

The family found miserable refuge in the cottage in Germany where I discovered them. The traitorous Turk showed no gratitude for the difficulty they had endured in trying to help him. When he heard that his rescuer faced poverty and ruin, he left Italy with his daughter, insulting Felix by sending him a small sum of money to assist him.

The events preyed on Felix's heart, and made him the most miserable member of his family when I first saw him. He could have endured poverty, and gloried in the hardship as the price of his virtue, but the Turk's betrayal and the loss of his bellowed Safie were bitter misfortunes and harder for him to bear. The arrival of the Arabian put new life into his soul.

When the Turk heard that Felix had lost his wealth and position, he ordered his daughter to forget her lover and prepare to return to her native country. Safie's generous nature was outraged by this command. She tried to plead with her father, but her words only made her father angry, and he repeated his order.

A few days later, Safie's father came to her rooms and told her that his residence in Leghorn had been discovered, and French officials were coming to seize him. He had hired a ship to take him to Constantinople, and he would leave in a few hours. He planned to leave his daughter under the care of a trusted servant. She could follow him later, bringing most of his property, which had not yet arrived at Leghorn.

Safie hated the idea of living in Turkey. Both her feelings and her religion opposed it. When her father had gone, she considered what she should do. Looking through her father's papers, she learned about Felix's exile and the name of the place where he was living. Safie hesitated while she considered her decision, but she finally came to a determination. She took some money and jewels that belonged to her and departed for Germany. She was attended by a native of Leghorn who understood the language of Turkey.

Safie arrived safely at a town about twenty leagues from the De Lacey cottage, when her attendant became dangerously ill. Although Safie nursed her with devoted affection, the poor girl died. The Arabian found herself left alone in a strange place where she did not know the language. Fortunately, she met with kindness. The woman of the house where they were staying took care that Safie should safely reach the cottage of her lover.

Chapter 15

Such was the history of my beloved cottagers. I was deeply impressed by their story. From this view of social life, I learned to admire their virtues and condemn the vices of humankind.

Up to this point, kindness and generosity were always present around me, and crime seemed like some distant evil. I was filled with the desire to participate in the busy scene of life which revealed so many admirable qualities. But, as I describe the progress of my thinking, I must not leave out something that happened at the beginning of August that same year.

One night, I had gone out, making my usual visit to the nearby wood where I collected my own food and gathered firewood for my protectors. I found a leather trunk on the ground that contained several items of clothing and some books. I seized the prize eagerly and carried it back to my hovel. Fortunately, the books were written in the language I had learned to understand at the cottage. The books included *Paradise Lost,* a volume of Plutarch's *Lives,* and the *Sorrows of Werter.* I was delighted to own these treasures, and I studied and examined these histories constantly while my friends were busy with their usual occupations.

The books filled me with a multitude of new feelings and images that raised me to ecstasy, but more often sunk me into the lowest despair. I can hardly describe their effect on me. In addition to its simple, touching story, *Sorrows of Werter* explored many different points of view and illuminated subjects I had found difficult to understand before. I found it a never-ending source for contemplation and astonishment. It described gentle, domestic scenes combined with lofty feelings and ideals, which reminded me of my own experience living among my protectors, and the desires alive in my own heart. But, Werter seemed to be a divine being, unlike anyone I had met or imagined. He had depth without pride. I was fascinated by the discussion about death and suicide. I did not pretend to understand the arguments, but I tended to agree with the hero. I wept over his death without precisely understanding it.

I applied what I read to my own feelings and situation. I found myself similar, yet strangely unlike, the beings in the books, and the beings I observed as a listener. I sympathized with them, and partly understood them, but my mind was unformed. I related to nobody and depended on nobody. 'The path of my departure was free,' and nobody would grieve over my death. My appearance was hideous, and my size was gigantic. What did this mean? Who was I? What was I? Where did I come from? Where was I going? I thought about these questions constantly, but I could not answer them.

The volume of Plutarch that I had found described the first founders of the ancient republics. This book affected me very differently than *Sorrows of Werter*. I learned to visualize gloom and despair from Werter's imagination. But, Plutarch taught me about high ideals, and he raised me above the wretched sphere of my own thoughts. I grew to love and admire the heroes of past ages. Many of the things I read exceeded my understanding and experience. I had only vague understanding of kingdoms, wide extents of country, mighty rivers, and boundless seas. But, I was well-acquainted with towns and large groups of people. So far, I had studied human nature in the cottage of my protectors, but this book showed me new and mightier scenes of action. I read about men who were concerned with public affairs, who ruled or massacred their fellow human beings. I felt the greatest love for virtue and hatred for vice rising within me, as far as I could understand those terms. Virtue and vice seemed to resemble pleasure and pain to me. Motivated by these feelings, I admired the peaceful lawgivers Numa, Solon, and Lycurgus, and preferred them to Romulus and Theseus. The peaceful lives of my protectors strengthened the impression on my mind. It is possible that I would have felt differently if my first introduction to humanity had been a young solder burning for glory and slaughter.

Paradise Lost inspired different and far deeper emotions. I thought *Paradise* Lost, and all the books, described true events. I was overwhelmed by wonder and awe when I imagined an omnipotent God at war with his creatures. I often compared the things I read in books to my own life. Like me, Adam had not come from any other being in existence, otherwise his situation was completely different from mine. God had made him to be a perfect, happy, prosperous creature, and his Creator guarded him with special care. He was allowed to speak with superior beings, and learn from them, but I was wretched, helpless, and alone. I often thought that I resembled Satan more than Adam. Like Satan, I was filled with bitter envy when I considered the happiness of my protectors.

Something else happened that strengthened and confirmed my feelings. Soon after I arrived at the hovel, I found some papers in the pocket of the clothes I had taken from your laboratory. At first I had ignored them, but now that I could read, I began to study them with diligence. It was your journal of the four months before my creation. You recorded every step you took in the progress of your work. Everyday events were mixed with this record. I am sure you remember these papers – here they are. They describe everything that relates to my cursed origin, the whole series of disgusting circumstances that led to my creation. You describe my loathsome, repulsive appearance in minute detail, and I will never forget the language you used to convey your horror. I felt sick as I read the papers. 'Hateful day when I received life!' I exclaimed in agony. 'Cursed creator! Why did you make a monster so hideous that even YOU turned away from me in disgust? God was merciful, and made human beings beautiful in his own image. But, my form is a filthy copy of yours, and the very resemblance makes it more horrible.

Even Satan had fellow devils for companions to admire and encourage him, but I am hated and alone.'

I could not help thinking this way during my hours of solitude and despair. When I considered the kind, virtuous nature of the cottagers, I convinced myself that they would show compassion towards me and overlook my deformity, once they knew how much I admired them. If I came to their door, asking for compassion and friendship, could they turn me away, no matter how monstrous I appeared? I determined not to give in to despair, but to prepare myself in every way to meet them. I delayed the attempt for some months longer. This meeting would decide my fate, and I dreaded failure. Besides, I found that I could understand more every day, and I was reluctant to try until I had gained more knowledge.

Several changes took place in the cottage. Safie's presence brought happiness to everyone, and the cottagers seemed to enjoy a greater degree of plenty. Felix and Agatha spent more time talking and enjoying themselves, and servants helped with their work. They were not rich, but they seemed happy and content. Their feelings were calm and peaceful, while my feelings became more tumultuous every day. The more I learned, the more I realized what a wretched outcast I was. My hope vanished when I saw my reflection in the water, or my shadow in the moonshine.

I tried to crush my fears, and make myself stronger for the challenge I would face in a few months. Sometimes I dared to imagine that the lovely, kind creatures would sympathize with my feelings and cheer my gloom. Their angelic faces would smile and comfort me. But, it was all a dream. No Eve shared my thoughts or soothed my sorrow, I was alone. I remembered Adam pleading with his Creator. Where was my creator? He had abandoned me, and I cursed him from the bitterness of my heart.

Autumn passed away. I was sorry and surprised to see the leaves decay and fall. Nature looked bleak and barren as it had appeared when I first saw the woods and the lovely moon. I did not mind the bleakness of the weather because I found it easier to tolerate cold than heat. But, I had found delight in the flowers and birds, and the lovely appearance of summer. When the beauty of summer deserted me, I turned with greater attention to the cottagers. Their happiness was not diminished by the change of season. They had love and sympathy for one another. Their joys depended on each other, and it was not affected by the weather. The more I observed them, the more I longed to claim their protection and kindness. My heart yearned to be known and loved by these kind creatures. My greatest wish was to have their sweet, affectionate looks directed at me. I did not allow myself to think that they would turn away from me with horror and disgust. They never turned away the poor people who came to their door. It is true that I was asking for something more valuable than food and rest, I was asking for their kindness and sympathy. But, I did not believe I was unworthy of the treasure.

The winter progressed. A full year had passed since I awoke into life. All my attention was focused on my plan for introducing myself to my protectors. I considered many different plans, but I finally decided to enter the cottage when the blind old man was alone. I knew that my hideous, unnatural appearance was the main thing that horrified the first people who saw me. My voice was harsh, but it was not terrible. I thought if I could gain old De Lacey's good will, he might mediate with his children, and they would tolerate me.

One day, Safie, Agatha, and Felix left for a long walk in the country. The sun shone cheerfully on the red leaves that covered the ground, though it did not provide much warmth. The old man chose to remain alone in the cottage. When his children had gone, he picked up his guitar and played several sweet, sad tunes. I had never heard him play such sweet, sad music. At first, he seemed happy, but as he continued to play, his expression became sad and thoughtful. He finally put aside his instrument and became absorbed in thought.

My heart beat quickly. This was the moment and hour of my trial, which would realize my hopes or my fears. The servants had gone to a nearby fair. The cottage was silent, and it was an excellent opportunity, yet my limbs trembled and I sank to the ground. I mustered all my energy and rose, removing the planks that I had placed in front of the entrance to my hovel. The fresh air revived me, and I approached the door of the cottage with renewed determination.

I knocked, and the old man said, 'Who is there? Come in.'

'Pardon this intrusion,' I said, and entered. 'I am a traveler. Would you allow me to rest for a few minutes before your fire?'

'Enter,' De Lacey said, 'and I will see how I can help you. Unfortunately, my children are away from home, and I am blind. I am afraid I will find it difficult to find food for you.'

'Do not trouble yourself, my kind host. I have food, I only need rest and warmth.'

I sat down, and we were silent. I knew that every moment was precious, yet I was unsure how to begin the conversation. The old man addressed me and said, 'By your language, stranger, I guess that you are my countryman, and you are French?'

'No, but I was educated by a French family, and it is the only language I understand. Now I am on my way to claim the protection of some friends. I love them sincerely, and hope for their favor.'

'Are they German?'

'No, they are French. But, let us talk about something else. I am a deserted, unfortunate creature. I have no relation or friend in the world. The kind people I am going to find have never seen me and know little about me. I am afraid. If I fail with them, I will be outcast in the world forever.'

'Do not despair. It is indeed unfortunate to be friendless. But, human hearts are full of brotherly love and charity, when they are not motivated by obvious self-interest. Rely on your hopes. If these friends are good and kind, do not despair.'

'They are kind – they are the best people in the world. But, unfortunately, they are prejudiced against me. I have good character, and I have harmed nobody, I have tried to be helpful. But, a fatal prejudice closes their eyes, and they do not see me as a kind, feeling friend, instead they see a detestable monster.'

'That is unfortunate indeed, but if you are really blameless, can you not convince them?'

'I am about to try, and that is the reason I feel such overwhelming fear. I dearly love these friends. Unknown to them, I have helped them every day for many months. But, they believe that I want to hurt them, and I would like to overcome this prejudice.'

'Where do these friends live?'

'Near this spot.'

The old man paused, and then continued, 'If you tell me the details of your story, perhaps I can help you convince them. I am blind, and I cannot judge your appearance, but your words sound sincere. I am exiled and poor, but it would please me to help a fellow human creature.'

'Excellent man! I thank you, and I accept your generous offer. You raise me from the dust with this kindness. I trust that with your help I will not be driven from the kindness and society of your fellow creatures.'

'Heaven forbid! Even if you were really criminal, removing you from society would only drive you to desperation, not motivate you to good behavior. I am unfortunate, and my family was also condemned, though we are innocent. We can feel for your misfortune.'

'How can I thank you, my best and only friend? From you, I have heard the voice of kindness directed to me for the first time. I will be grateful to you forever, and your humanity assures me that I will be successful with the friends I am about to meet.'

'Can you tell me the names of your friends and their address?'

I paused and reflected that this was the moment of decision, which would endow me with happiness or take it away forever. Struggling to find the strength to answer him, I sank down on the chair and sobbed out loud. I heard the footsteps of my younger protectors. I did not have a moment to lose. Grasping the old man's hand, I cried, 'Now is the time! Save and protect me! You and your family are the friends that I seek. Do not desert me in this hour of need.'

'Great God!' the old man exclaimed. 'Who are you?'

At that instant, the cottage door opened, and Felix, Safie, and Agatha came inside. Who can describe their shock and horror at seeing me? Agatha fainted, and Safie ran out of the cottage, unable to help her friend. I clung to the old man's knees, and Felix darted forward and pulled me away from his father with supernatural strength. Overcome with fury, he threw me to the ground and struck me violently with a stick. I could have torn him apart, as a lion tears an antelope, but I restrained myself. I felt bitterly heartsick. Felix was about to repeat the blow, when I ran from the cottage, overwhelmed by anguish and pain, and retreated to my hovel amid the commotion.

Chapter 16

Cursed, cursed creator! Why did I live? Why didn't I extinguish the spark of life you had so carelessly bestowed? I don't know the reason. I felt rage and the desire for revenge. I was not yet overcome by despair. I could have destroyed the cottage and its inhabitants with pleasure, and I would have enjoyed their shrieks and misery.

When night came, I left my retreat and wandered in the wood. I was no longer restrained by the fear of discovery, and I howled out loud in my anguish. I was like a wild animal that had broken its chains. I ran through the wood with the swiftness of a deer, destroying the objects that blocked my path. I passed a miserable night. The bare trees waved their branches above me, and the cold stars mocked me. From time to time, the sweet voice of a bird burst forth amid the general stillness. Everyone except me enjoyed some pleasure or rest. Like the arch-fiend, I carried hell within me. Finding no sympathy, I wished to tear up the trees, spread ruin, and destroy everything around me. I would have enjoyed sitting down among the ruins.

I could not endure my sensations for long. Exhausted by my physical exertion, I sank down on the damp grass. I felt sick with impotent despair. Not one man among the thousands would help or pity me. Why should I feel kindness towards my enemies? From that moment, I declared everlasting war against the human species, most of all against the man who had created me and left me to face this unbearable misery.

The sun rose, and I heard people's voices. I knew that I could not return to my retreat that day. I hid myself in some thick undergrowth and spent the next hours considering my situation.

The pure air and pleasant sunshine made me feel more peaceful. When I considered what had happened at the cottage, I could not help thinking I had been too hasty in my conclusions.

I had not acted carefully enough. The father had clearly felt sympathy for me. I was a fool to expose myself to the horror of his children. I should have made myself familiar to old De Lacey gradually, and slowly introduced myself to the rest of his family, when they were prepared to meet me. I did not believe my mistake was final. After much thought, I decided to return to the cottage, find the old man, and present my case.

I became calmer and fell into a deep sleep in the afternoon. I was still too excited to have peaceful dreams. The horrible scene from yesterday replayed itself in my mind. The females ran from me, and Felix tore me away from his father. I woke up feeling exhausted and found that it was already night. I crawled out of my hiding place and went in search of food.

When my hunger was satisfied, I followed the familiar path towards the cottage. Everything was quiet. I crept into my hovel and waited silently for the usual hour when the family awoke. The sun rose high in the sky, and the cottagers did not appear. I shivered violently, fearing some dreadful misfortune. The cottage was dark and nothing moved. I cannot describe the agony of my suspense.

After some time, two countrymen approached along the road. They paused near the cottage and entered into conversation, gesturing wildly with their hands. I did not understand their language, which was different from the language of my protectors, but Felix soon approached with another man. I had not seen him leave the cottage that morning, and I waited, anxious to learn what had happened.

'You do realize,' the other man said, 'you will have to pay three months' rent, and you will lose the produce of your garden? I don't want to take advantage. I think you should take a few days to consider your decision.'

'It is useless,' Felix replied, 'we can never live in your cottage again. My father's health is in danger from the shock. My wife and my sister will never recover from their horror. I beg you not to argue with me any more. Take back your cottage and let me leave this place.'

Felix trembled as he said these words. He went inside the cottage with the other man, and they stayed inside for a few minutes, then they left. I never saw the De Lacey family again.

I stayed in my hovel for the rest of the day in a state of stupefying despair. My protectors had left and broken the only link that connected me to the world. For the first time, I allowed my feelings of hatred and revenge to take control of my heart. I turned my thoughts towards injury and death. I forgot my violent thoughts when I considered my friends, De Lacey's mild voice, Agatha's gentle eyes, and the exquisite beauty of the Arabian. I felt soothed by my tears. When I remembered that they had rejected and deserted me, my rage and anger returned. Unable to injure another human being, I turned my fury on the objects around me. When night came, I piled material that would burn around the cottage and destroyed every trace of cultivation in the garden. I waited impatiently for the moon to set.

As it grew late, a fierce wind arose from the woods and blew away the clouds that lingered in the night sky. The blast of wind produced a kind of insanity in my spirits that burst forth beyond all reason and reflection. I lighted the dry branch of a tree and danced furiously around the deserted cottage. I kept my eyes fixed on the western sky where the moon was setting. As it moved below the horizon, I held up my flaming brand. With a loud scream, I set fire to the straw and brush and bushes I had collected. The wind fanned the fire, and the cottage was quickly engulfed by tongues of flame.

As soon as I was sure that the cottage was beyond saving, I left the scene and took refuge in the woods.

Now, with the world before me, where should I go? I was determined to leave the scene of my misfortune, but, hated and despised as I was, every place would be equally horrible to me. At last, the thought of you crossed my mind. I had learned

111

from your papers that you were my father, my creator, and it seemed right that I should appeal to the person who had given me life. Felix had included geography in his lessons for Safie. From his lessons, I had learned about the relative location of the different countries. You had mentioned Geneva as the name of your native town, and I resolved to go there.

But, how could I know which way to go? I knew that I must travel in a southwesterly direction to reach my destination, but the sun was my only guide. I did not know the names of the towns I must pass through, and I could not ask a single human being for information. Even so, I did not despair. You were the only person I could go to for help, though I felt nothing but hatred for you. Unfeeling, heartless creator! You had endowed me with thoughts and feelings and then cast me out into the world to face the scorn and horror of humankind. I could appeal only to you for pity and help. I had determined to seek the justice from you that I had vainly tried to gain from other human beings.

I traveled for a long time, and endured intense suffering. It was autumn when I left the place where I had lived for so long. I traveled only at night, fearful of meeting human beings. Nature decayed around me, and the sun no longer gave heat. Rain and snow poured down, mighty rivers froze, the surface of the earth was hard, bare, and chill, and I found no shelter. Oh, earth! How often did I curse the cause of my being? The mildness of my nature was transformed into gall and bitterness. I felt the spirit of revenge kindle more deeply in my heart, the closer I came to your home. Snow fell and waters turned to ice, but I did not rest. I had a map of the country, and some chance incidents directed me, but I often wandered far from my path. The agony of my feelings did not allow me to rest. My rage and misery were fed by everything around me, but one incident occurred when I reached the borders of Switzerland that especially confirmed the bitterness and horror of my feelings.

The sun had grown warm, and the earth was beginning to look green again. I generally rested during the day and traveled only at night when darkness concealed me from human sight. One morning, when I was walking through a deep wood, I continued with my journey after the sun rose. It was one of the first days of spring, and I was cheered by the mild temperature and lovely sunshine. I felt emotions of gentleness and pleasure, which had seemed long dead, revive within me. Half surprised by the novelty of my feelings, I allowed myself to be carried away by my emotions. Forgetting my solitude and deformity, I dared to be happy. Soft tears wet my cheeks, and I even raised my eyes with thankfulness towards the sun which brought me such joy.

I continued to follow the winding path until I reached the edge of the wood, which skirted a deep, rapidly flowing river. The trees bent their budding branches towards the water. I paused, uncertain which way to go, when I heard the sound of voices and hid beneath the shade of a cypress tree. I had scarcely concealed myself, when a young girl came running towards my hiding place. She was laughing, as if she was running away from somebody in fun. She ran along the steep riverbank until, suddenly, her foot slipped and she fell into the rapid stream. I rushed out from my hiding place. Fighting the force of the current with great effort, I dragged her to the shore and saved her. She was unconscious. I tried everything I could to revive her, when I was interrupted by a countryman, who was probably the person she had playfully run from. On seeing me, he ran forward, tore the girl from my arms, and ran towards the deeper part of the wood. I followed at great speed, hardly knowing the reason I followed them. When the man saw me come close, he aimed his gun at my body and fired. I sank to the ground, and the man who had injured me escaped quickly into the wood.

This was the reward for my kindness! I had saved a human being from destruction, and in return I now writhed from the miserable pain of a wound that shattered flesh and bone.

The feeling of kindness I had experienced just a few moments before now turned to hellish rage. Inflamed by pain, I vowed eternal hatred and vengeance on all humankind. But, the agony of my wound overcame my consciousness, my pulse grew weak, and I fainted.

For the next few weeks, I lived a miserable existence in the woods, trying to cure my wound. The bullet had entered my shoulder, and I had no idea whether it had passed through my shoulder or still remained there. In any case, I had no way to remove it. My suffering was increased by the oppressive sense of the ingratitude and injustice of my injury. Every day I vowed revenge, deep and deadly revenge, that would make up for the anguish and outrage I had endured.

After some weeks, my wound healed, and I continued my journey. I was no longer encouraged by the bright sun and gentle breezes of spring. Joy simply mocked my desolate condition, and made me more painfully aware that I was not created to enjoy pleasure.

At last, my journey came to an end, and two months later I reached the vicinity of Geneva.

I arrived in the evening and retreated to a hiding place in the fields to consider how I should approach you. I was oppressed by fatigue and hunger, and I was much too unhappy to enjoy the gentle breeze of evening or the view of the sun setting behind the stupendous mountains of Jura.

Sleep relieved the pain of thinking, until my sleep was interrupted by the approach of a beautiful child who ran into my hiding place. Seeing him, it occurred to me that perhaps this little creature had not yet learned to hate deformity. If I could keep him with me, and teach him to be my companion and friend, I would not be so alone in the world.

Moved by this impulse, I seized the boy and pulled him close to me. As soon as he saw my appearance, he covered his eyes with his hands and uttered a shrill scream. I pulled his hand away from his face and said, 'Child, what do you mean? I am not going to hurt you, listen to me.'

He struggled violently. 'Let me go!' he cried. 'Monster! Ugly wretch! You want to tear me to pieces and eat me. You are an ogre! Let me go, or I will tell my Papa!'

'Boy, you will never see your father again. You must come with me.'

'Hideous monster! Let me go – my father works for the government. He is Monsieur Frankenstein – he will punish you. You do not dare to keep me.'

'Frankenstein! You belong to my enemy – I have sworn eternal revenge against him. You will be my first victim.'

The child still struggled and cursed me using words that filled my heart with despair. I grasped his throat to silence him, and in a moment he lay dead at my feet.

I gazed at my victim, and my heart swelled with joy and hellish triumph. I clapped my hands and exclaimed, 'I can create destruction too. My enemy is not invincible. This death will hurt him, and I will torment and destroy him with a thousand other miseries.'

As I stared at the child, I saw something glittering around his neck. I took it out and saw that it was the portrait of a lovely woman. It softened and attracted me in spite of my dark thoughts. For a few moments, I gazed with delight at her dark eyes, fringed by deep lashes, and her lovely lips. Then my rage returned when I recalled that I was forever deprived of the company of such beautiful creatures. If this woman saw me, her expression of divine kindness would change to horror and disgust.

Are you surprised that such thoughts filled me with rage? I am only surprised that I vented my feelings in exclamations and agony. I did not rush out and kill myself trying to destroy humankind.

Overcome by my feelings, I left the place where I had committed the murder and looked for a more secluded hiding place. I entered a barn which seemed to be empty. A young woman was sleeping on the straw. She was not as beautiful as the woman in the picture, but she was pretty and blooming with health and youth. I reflected that she was another creature who brought joy to everyone besides me. I bent over her and whispered, 'Awake, fair one, your lover is near. He would give his life for one look of affection from you. Awake, my beloved!'

The sleeper moved, and a thrill of terror ran through me. What would happen if she actually woke, and saw me, and cursed me, and denounced me as the murderer? She would surely denounce me if she opened her dark eyes and saw me. The thought brought madness and stirred the fiend within me. I would not suffer, she should suffer. I had committed the murder because I was forever robbed of everything she could give me, and she would pay. She was the source of the crime, and she would face the punishment. I had learned about human laws from the lessons of Felix, and now I knew how to cause trouble. I bent over her and placed the portrait securely in one of the folds of her dress. She moved again, and I ran.

For some days I lingered in the spot where these events had taken place. Sometimes I wished to see you, and sometimes I determined to leave the world and its miseries forever. I finally wandered towards these mountains, and I have ranged through their immense valleys, consumed by burning passion which you alone can satisfy. You cannot leave until you agree to grant my request. I am alone and miserable. No human being will associate with me, but someone as deformed and horrible as myself would not reject me. My companion must belong to the same species as myself and have the same defects. You must create this being."

∞∞∞∞∞∞∞∞∞∞∞∞∞∞∞∞∞∞∞

Chapter 17

The creature finished speaking and looked at me, expecting a reply. But, I was confused and did not know how to respond to his proposition. He continued, "You must create a female for me so that I can live with her. You alone can do it, and I demand it from you as a right which you must not refuse."

My anger had died away while he described his peaceful life among the cottagers, but anger had kindled anew when I listened to the final part of his story. As he spoke, I could no longer suppress the rage that burned within me.

"I do refuse," I replied, "No torture will make me agree. You can make me the most miserable man in existence, but you will never make me lower myself in my own eyes. Do you think I will create another being like you, when your joint wickedness might desolate the world? Begone! You have my answer. You can torture me, but I will never agree."

"You are wrong," the fiend replied. "Instead of threatening, I am content to reason with you. I am malicious because I am miserable. Am I not hated and rejected by humankind? You, my creator, would tear me to pieces and feel triumph. Remember that, and tell me why I should pity humankind more than it pities me? You would not call it murder if you could throw me down into one of those icy valleys and destroy my frame, the work of your own hands. Should I respect human beings when they condemn me? Let people show me kindness, and I will not injure them. I will respond with tears of gratitude at their acceptance. But, that is not possible. Human senses form a barrier to our union that is impossible to overcome. Yet, I will not submit myself to abject slavery. I will revenge my injuries. If I cannot inspire love, then I will inspire fear. I will swear undying hatred towards you, my arch-enemy, because you are my creator. Take care, I will work towards your destruction, and I will not stop until I desolate your heart, so that you curse the hour you were born."

Fiendish rage animated him as he spoke, and his face wrinkled into contortions too horrible for human eyes to behold. But, he calmed himself and continued –

"I intended to reason with you. This emotion hurts me, because you do not consider that YOU are the cause of my excess feeling. If any being showed me kindness, I would return their feeling one hundred times. For the sake of that one creature, I would make peace with the whole of humankind! But, that is a dream of happiness that will never be. What I ask you is reasonable and moderate. I ask you to make a female creature as hideous as myself. It is the only happiness possible for me, and I will be content. It is true that we will be monsters and cut off from the world. But, our isolation will make us more attached to each other. Our lives will not be happy, but we will be harmless and free from the misery I feel now. Oh! My creator, make me happy. Let me feel gratitude towards you for one kindness. Let me feel the sympathy of one living being. Do not deny my request!"

I was moved. I shuddered when I considered the possible consequences if I agreed with his request. But, I felt there was some justice in his argument. His story and the thoughts he expressed proved that he was a creature of fine feelings. As his creator, did I not owe him all the happiness it was in my power to give? He noticed the change in my feelings and continued –

'If you agree, then neither you nor any other human being will ever see us again. I will go to the vast wild lands of South America. I do not eat the same food as human beings. I do not destroy the young lamb and goat to satisfy my appetite. Acorns and berries give me nourishment. My companion will be content with the same food. We will make our bed from dried leaves. The sun will shine on us, just as it does on human beings,

118

and it will ripen our food. I describe to you a scene that is peaceful and human. You must feel that you could deny it only through wanton power and cruelty. You have been pitiless towards me, but now I see compassion in your eyes. Let me take this moment to persuade you to promise what I sincerely desire."

"You propose to live far from human beings," I replied, "where the animals will be your only companions. How can you exist in exile, when you long for the love and sympathy of humankind? You will return and seek acceptance from people. Your evil passion will be renewed when they reject you, and you will have a companion to help you destroy them. This cannot happen, do not argue with me, I cannot agree."

"Your feelings are so inconsistent! Just a moment ago, you were moved by my story. Why do you harden yourself against me? I swear to you, by the earth where I live, and by you who created me, that I will live in the most remote places with the companion you give me. My evil passions will vanish, because I will have sympathy! My life will flow away quietly, and I will not curse my maker in my dying moments."

His words had a strange effect on me. I felt compassion for him, and sometimes I wanted to comfort him. But, when I looked at him and saw the filthy mass that moved and spoke, my heart grew sick, and my feelings changed to horror and hatred. I tried to stifle these emotions. Since I could not give him my own sympathy, I thought I had no right to deny him the small portion of happiness that was still in my power to give.

"You promise to be harmless," I said, "but doesn't your evil behavior makes it reasonable for me to distrust you? What if this is a trick to increase your triumph and expand your scope for revenge?"

"What do you mean? I must not be trifled with, and I demand an answer. If I have no affection and no ties to the world, then hatred and evil must be my portion. Having the love of another being will destroy the cause of my crimes. Nobody will know that I exist. My evil behavior comes from my forced solitude. My virtues will arise when I have the companionship of somebody who is my equal. I will feel the affection of a sensitive being, and I will be joined to the chain of existence from which I am excluded."

I paused for some time to think about everything he had said, and consider his various arguments. I thought about the promise of virtue he had shown when he first came into existence, and how his kindly feelings were blighted by the loathing and scorn his protectors had shown him. I did not ignore his strength and his threats. It would be useless to fight against the power of a being who could live in the icy caves of the glaciers and hide himself among the mountain peaks. After thinking for a long time, I decided that I owed justice both to him and my fellow creatures, and I should agree with his request. I turned to him and said –

"I agree with your demand, as long as you solemnly promise to leave Europe forever and stay far away from human beings, as soon as I give you a female to go with you into exile."

"I swear," he cried, "by the sun, by the blue sky of heaven, and by the fire of love that lights my heart. While they exist, you will never see me again if you grant my prayer. Depart to your home, and begin your work. I will watch your progress with unspeakable anxiety. When you are ready, I will appear."

He suddenly left me, perhaps fearful that I would change my mind. I saw him descend the glacier faster than an eagle can fly, and I quickly lost sight of him within the rising and falling sea of ice.

It had taken the whole day to tell his story, and the sun was just setting when he left me. I knew that I should climb down quickly towards the valley because I would soon be surrounded by darkness. But, my heart was heavy, and my steps were slow. I found it difficult to follow the small, winding mountain paths, after the emotions of the day. Night was far advanced when I reached the resting-place beside the mountain. The stars shone from time to time as the clouds passed over them. The dark pines rose before me, and broken trees lay scattered on the ground. The scene was wonderfully solemn, and it stirred strange thoughts within me. I wept bitterly and clasped my hands in agony. "Oh!" I exclaimed. "Stars and clouds and winds, you have all come to mock me. If you really pity me, crush my memory and feelings, and let me turn into nothing. If not, then leave me, leave me in darkness."

These were wild, miserable thoughts, but I cannot describe to you how the eternal twinkling of the stars weighed on me, and how I listened to every blast of the wind as if it was a dull, ugly force coming to destroy me.

Morning dawned before I arrived at the village of Chamounix. I did not rest, but returned immediately to Geneva. I could not express my feelings even to myself. My emotions pressed on me with the weight of a mountain, and my agony was crushed beneath their weight. In this condition, I returned home and presented myself to my family. My wild, haggard appearance alarmed them, but I did not answer their questions, I scarcely spoke. I felt as though I was placed under a ban, and I had no right to claim their sympathy. I felt that I could never again enjoy their company. Even so, I loved them dearly, and in order to save them I resolved to dedicate myself to my hated task. The thought of this project seemed like the only real thing in my life, and everything else around me seemed like a dream.

∞∞∞∞∞∞∞∞∞∞∞∞∞∞∞∞∞∞∞∞

Chapter 18

Day after day, week after week, passed after my return to Geneva, and I could not summon the courage to begin my work. I feared the vengeance of the disappointed fiend. Yet, I could not overcome my revulsion for the task I was requested to do. I found that I could not create a female without devoting several months to dedicated study. I heard about some discoveries made by an English scientist, which might be important for my success, and I sometimes considered asking my father for permission to visit England for this purpose. But, I clung to every excuse for delay. I hesitated to take the first step to begin a project that seemed less necessary to me. A change had taken place in me. My health, which had previously declined, now improved, and my spirits rose likewise, when I was not checked by the memory of my unhappy promise. My father was happy to see this change. He considered the best way to eliminate the last traces of melancholy, which did return from time to time and overshadowed the approaching sunshine with devouring blackness. At these times, I took refuge in the most perfect solitude. I passed whole days alone on the lake in a little boat, silent and listless, watching the clouds and listening to the rippling of the waves. But, the fresh air and bright sun almost always restored my mood to some degree. Returning home, I would respond to the greetings of my family with a readier smile and more cheerful heart.

One day when I had returned from one of these rambles, my father called me aside and said –

"My dear son, I am glad to see that you have resumed your former activities, and you seem more like yourself. But, you are still unhappy, and you still avoid our company. For some time, I have wondered about the cause, but yesterday an idea occurred to me. You must tell me if my guess is correct.

122

Staying quiet about something so important would not simply be useless, it would bring misery to all of us."

I trembled violently when I heard his words. My father continued – "My son, I confess that I have always looked forward to your marriage to dear Elizabeth as the foundation of our domestic comfort, and the support of my declining years. You were attached to each other from your earliest childhood, you studied together, and your personalities seemed entirely suited to one another. But, perhaps I was mistaken. Perhaps you have regarded Elizabeth as your sister and you do not want her to be your wife. You might have met somebody else whom you love, but you consider yourself bound in honor to Elizabeth. The struggle might cause the acute misery you seem to feel."

"My dear father, you can feel assured that I love my cousin tenderly and sincerely. I have never met another woman who inspires my admiration and affection as Elizabeth does. My future hopes are completely bound up in the expectation of our marriage."

"My dear Victor, your words make me happier than I have felt for some time. If you feel this way, we can be happy, no matter how gloomy things seem at the moment. I would like to dispel the gloom that has taken such strong hold of your mind. Do you object if the marriage takes place soon? We have been unlucky, and recent events have disturbed the peace that suits my age and health. You are young. But, you have a reasonable fortune, and I do not think that marrying early would interfere with any plans you might have for work or future achievement. Do not imagine that I am trying to tell you what to do. I will understand if you prefer to wait. I am speaking with you openly. You can answer me honestly and tell me what you feel."

I listened to my father in silence, and for some time I could not speak. A multitude of thoughts went through my mind, and I tried to find some response. Alas! The thought of marrying my Elizabeth filled me with horror and dismay. I was bound by a solemn promise which I had not yet fulfilled, and did not dare to break. If I did break the promise, what miseries might my family face? Could I celebrate, with this weight still hanging around my neck and bowing me to the ground? I must complete my task and let the monster depart with his mate, before I could allow myself to enjoy this marriage which I hoped would bring me peace.

I recalled that I would need to travel to England, or correspond with scientists there, to gain more knowledge to complete my project. Corresponding by letter was slow and unsatisfactory. Besides, I was reluctant to work on my loathsome task while living in my father's house with the family I loved. I knew that a thousand accidents might happen, and the slightest accident would reveal this story that would horrify everybody who knew me. I was also aware that I would often lose all self-control. I would lose all capacity to hide the harrowing sensations that would possess me during the progress of my unearthly work. I must stay away from the people I loved while I worked on my project. Once I began, it would quickly be finished, and I could return to my family to live in peace and happiness. Once my promise was fulfilled, the monster would depart forever. Or (I could hope) some accident might happen in the meantime that would destroy him and end my slavery forever.

These feelings guided the answer I gave my father. I expressed my desire to visit England but concealed the real reason for my request. I stated my request in a way that excited no suspicion. At the same time, I described how much I wished to go, and easily moved my father to agree. After watching me suffer for so long from intense depression that resembled madness in its effects, he was glad to find that I was looking forward to traveling. He hoped that the amusement and change of scene would help me recover completely before I returned.

I would determine how long I stayed. I might stay for a few months or at most one year. My father took the kind precaution of making sure I had a companion. Without letting me know, he and Elizabeth had arranged for Clerval to join me at Strasbourg. This interfered with the solitude I wanted to work on my project. Yet, the presence of my friend would not interfere with anything at the beginning of my journey, and truly I rejoiced that I was saved from many hours of lonely, maddening thought. Perhaps Henry would stand between me and the intrusion of my enemy. If I was alone, he might force his hated presence upon me to remind me of my task or ask about its progress.

I left for England, and it was agreed that my marriage to Elizabeth would take place as soon as I returned. My father's age made him extremely reluctant to delay. For myself, I promised myself one reward when I had completed my hated work, one consolation for my unparalleled sufferings. When I was released from my miserable slavery, I might marry Elizabeth and forget about the past.

As I made the arrangements for my journey, one feeling haunted me and filled me with fear and agitation. While I was away, I would leave my family unaware that my enemy existed and unprotected from his attacks. My departure might provoke him. But, he had promised to follow me wherever I might go, perhaps he would follow me to England? This thought was dreadful in itself, but still it would be a relief since my family would stay safe. I was agonized when I imagined the opposite might happen. But, during the whole period of time when I was a slave to my creature, I allowed my actions to be ruled by the impulse of the moment. My present feelings strongly suggested that the fiend would follow me, and my family would be protected from the danger of his evil plan.

I left my native country for the second time at the end of September. The journey was my own idea, and Elizabeth had agreed, but she was worried about my suffering grief and misery while I was away from her. Men are blind to the thousand tiny details that women notice and attend with care. It was her suggestion to send Clerval as my companion. She wanted to tell me to return quickly, but a thousand conflicting emotions kept her silent as she tearfully bade me farewell.

I threw myself into the carriage, hardly aware where I was going, and not caring what was happening around me. It filled me with anguish, but I had remembered to have my chemical instruments packed to go with me. I passed through many beautiful and majestic scenes, but my eyes saw nothing, and I was filled with dreary thoughts. I could only think about the reason for my travel, and the work that would occupy me.

After spending some days in this listless state, I arrived at Strasbourg, where I waited two days for Clerval. He arrived. Alas, how great was the difference between us! He was alive to every new scene. He was joyful when he saw the beauty of the setting sun, and even happier when he saw it rise and begin a new day. He pointed out the shifting colors of the landscape and the appearance of the sky. "This is what it means to live," he cried. "How I enjoy life! But you, my dear Frankenstein, why are you depressed and sorrowful?" It was true that I was occupied by gloomy thoughts. I neither saw the setting of the evening star nor the golden sunrise reflected in the Rhine. Clerval observed the scenery with feeling and delight. You, my friend, would enjoy reading Clerval's journal rather than listening to my thoughts. I was a miserable wretch, haunted by a curse that shut off every enjoyment.

We had agreed to travel down the Rhine in a boat from Strasbourg to Rotterdam, and from there we would sail for London. During this voyage, we passed many willowy islands and saw many beautiful towns. We stayed for one day at Mannheim, and on the fifth day after leaving Strasbourg we arrived at Mainz. The course of the Rhine below Mainz becomes much more picturesque. The river descends rapidly and winds through steep, beautiful hills. We saw many ruined castles, high and remote, standing on the edge of cliffs, surrounded by black woods. This part of the Rhine presents a varied landscape. In one spot you can see rugged hills and ruined castles overlooking tremendous cliffs, with the dark Rhine rushing below. Suddenly you turn and see flourishing vineyards with green, sloping banks, and busy towns along the winding river.

We traveled at harvest time and heard the workers singing as we glided down the stream. Depressed in mind, with spirits constantly agitated by gloomy thoughts, even I was pleased. As I lay at the bottom of the boat and gazed at the cloudless, blue sky, I seemed to breathe in tranquility that I had not felt for a long time. If I felt this way, who can describe Henry's feelings? He felt that he had been transported to fairy-land and enjoyed happiness seldom experienced by human beings. "I have seen the most beautiful scenes of my own country," he said. "I have visited the lakes of Lucerne and Uri, where the snowy mountains descend directly into the water. The black shade from the mountains might seem gloomy if not for the bright, green islands. I have seen the lake agitated by a storm when waves dashed with fury against the base of the mountain. The wind tore up whirlwinds of water, and I could picture water-spouts on the great ocean. I have seen the mountains of La Valais and the Pays de Vaud, but this country, Victor, pleases me more than all the others. The mountains of Switzerland are more strange and majestic, but there is charm in the banks of this divine river that I have never seen anywhere else. Look at that castle overhanging the cliff on that island, almost hidden by those lovely trees, and now that group of workers coming back from their vines, and that village half hidden by the mountain. Oh, surely the spirit that dwells here and guards this place has a soul more agreeable to humankind than the spirit that piles up the glaciers and retreats to the remote mountain peaks of our own country."

Clerval! Beloved friend! Even now it delights me to remember your words and give you the praise that you deserve. He was a being formed in the "very poetry of nature." His wild, enthusiastic imagination was grounded by the feelings of his heart. His soul overflowed with affection. Worldly-minded people would think his kind of devoted friendship exists only in imagination. But, even human sympathy was not enough to satisfy his eager mind. The scenery of nature, which some people simply regard with admiration, he loved with passion. Where does he now exist? Is this gentle, lovely being lost forever? Has this wonderful mind, so filled with imagination and ideas, which created a world that depended on him for its existence, has this mind perished? Does it exist now only in my memory? No, it cannot be. Your beautiful form has decayed, but your spirit still visits and comforts your unhappy friend.

Please excuse this expression of sorrow. My words pay small tribute to Henry's great soul, but they soothe my heart, which overflows with anguish when I remember him. I will continue with my story.

After Cologne we descended to the plans of Holland. We decided to travel over land the rest of the way, since the wind was against us, and the flow of the river was too gentle to help us. We no longer had the interest of beautiful scenery after this point, but we arrived in a few days at Rotterdam, and then traveled by sea to England. I first saw the white cliffs of Britain on a clear morning near the end of October. The banks of the Thames showed us a new scene. They were flat, but fertile, and almost every town reminded us of some story. We saw Tilbury Fort, and remembered the Spanish Armada, and Gravesend, Woolwich, and Greenwich, places I had heard about even in my country.

At last, we saw the many steeples of London, with St. Paul's towering over them all, and the Tower, famous in English histo

Chapter 19

We decided to stay for several months in the wonderful, celebrated city of London. Clerval wanted to correspond with the men of talent and genius who flourished at this time. But, my main interest was obtaining the information I needed to complete my promise. I quickly made use of the letters of introduction I had brought with me, addressed to the most distinguished scientists.

If this journey had taken place during my former days of study and happiness, I would have enjoyed it greatly. But, my existence seemed cursed. I only visited these people for the sake of the information they might give me about the subject that interested me so profoundly. Company irritated me. When I was alone, I could fill my mind with the sights of nature, Henry's voice calmed me, and I could cheat myself into temporary peace. But, busy, joyous, uninteresting faces brought despair back to my heart. I saw an impassable barrier placed between me and my fellow beings. This barrier was sealed with the blood of William and Justine. My soul was filled with anguish whenever I recalled the events connected with those names.

Clerval reminded me of my former self. He was curious, and anxious to learn and gain experience. He was endlessly amused and interested by the people we met and their different habits. He was also pursuing a goal he had long had in mind. His plan was to visit India. He felt that with his knowledge of Indian languages and society, he could assist the progress of European colonization and trade. He could further his plan only in Britain. He was constantly busy, and my depressed, sorrowful mind was the only check on his enjoyment. I did not want to interfere with his enjoyment. He was undisturbed by any care or bitter memory, and it was natural that he should enjoy this new scene of life. I tried to conceal my thoughts as much as possible. I often refused to go out with him, saying I had another appointment, so that I might remain alone. I now began to collect the materials I would need for my new creation, and this was like torture to me. Every thought related to my project was painful, every word I spoke about it caused my lips to tremble, and my heart to race.

After spending some months in London, we received a letter from a person who lived in Scotland, who had previously visited us in Geneva. He described the beauties of his native country, and asked if we might like to travel as far north as Perth where he lived. Clerval was eager to accept this invitation. Although I hated society, I did want to see the mountains and streams, and the wonderful works of Nature. We had arrived in England near the end of October, and it was now February. We decided to travel north the next month. We would not follow the great road to Edinburgh, instead we would visit Windsor, Oxford, Matlock, and the Cumberland lakes, and complete the tour at the end of July. I packed up my chemical instruments and the materials I had collected, resolving to finish my work in some remote place in the northern highlands of Scotland.

We left London on the 27th of March and stayed for a few days in Windsor, rambling in its beautiful forest. We had come from the mountains, and the majestic oaks, the game animals, and the herds of stately deer were new to us.

From there we traveled to Oxford. As we entered the city, we recalled the historical events that had taken place there one hundred and fifty years before. Charles I. had collected his forces here. This city had remained faithful to him after the whole nation had deserted him to take the side of Parliament and liberty. The memory of the unfortunate king and his companions, the agreeable Falkland, the arrogant Goring, his queen and son, made the city interesting to us. We were delighted to find that the spirit of ancient times still lived here. Even if we had not found enjoyment in our feelings about the past, we would have admired the beauty of the city. The colleges are ancient and picturesque, and the streets seem almost magnificent. The lovely Isis flows through verdant, green fields, and the wide, peaceful waters reflect the majestic towers and spires and domes which are visible among the aged trees.

I enjoyed this scene, although my enjoyment seemed bitter when I recalled the past and considered the future. I longed for peace and happiness. I was rarely unhappy when I was young. If I was ever overcome by boredom, the study of the best creations and discoveries of human beings, or the beauty of nature, would always interest my heart and brighten my spirits. But, I am a blasted tree, and the bolt has entered my soul. I felt then that I would just live long enough to become this wrecked, miserable example of humanity, the object of pity for others and intolerable to myself.

We stayed quite some time in Oxford, rambling throughout the neighborhood, and identifying all the spots of historical interest. Our expeditions were often extended by the things we saw. We visited the tomb of the famous Hampden and the field where that patriot fell. For a moment, my soul was lifted above its low, miserable fears to contemplate the divine ideas of liberty and self-sacrifice represented by these monuments. For an instant, I dared to shake off my chains and look around me with a free and lofty spirit. But, the iron had eaten into my flesh. Hopeless and trembling, I retreated into my miserable self once more.

We left Oxford reluctantly, and traveled to Matlock, which was our next destination. The countryside near this village resembled a smaller-scale version of Switzerland. The green hills were missing the white crown of the distant Alps which always accompanied the pine-covered mountains of my native country. We visited the wondrous cave and the natural science museum where the exhibits are displayed in the same way as the collections at Servox and Chamounix. I trembled when Henry

131

spoke the name of Chamounix, and left Matlock quickly since it now seemed associated with that terrible scene.

We journeyed northward from Derby and spent two months in Cumberland and Westmorland. I could now almost imagine that I was among the Swiss mountains. Small patches of snow still lingered on the northern sides of the mountains. The lakes and the dashing, rocky streams all seemed familiar to me. We also met some acquaintances here who almost cheated me into happiness. Clerval's delight was greater than mine. His mind expanded in the company of talented people. He discovered greater capacities and resources within himself than he had realized. "I could spend my life here," he said, "and I would scarcely miss Switzerland and the Rhine, living among these mountains."

But, he found that the traveler's life includes pain as well as enjoyment. His feelings are constantly being stretched. As soon as the traveler begins to sink into rest, he must leave the thing he is enjoying to consider something new, until he must turn his attention to something else again.

We had scarcely visited the various lakes of Cumberland and Westmorland, and we had begun to grow fond of some of the people we had met, when it was time to meet our Scotch friend. I was not sorry to leave. I had now neglected my promise for some time, and I feared the demon's disappointment. He might have remained in Switzerland so he could wreak his vengeance on my family. This idea pursued me and tormented me during every moment when I might have taken some rest. I waited for my letters with feverish impatience. If the letters were delayed, I was miserable and overcome by a thousand fears. When they arrived, and I saw the address written by my father or Elizabeth, I hardly dared to read and learn what had happened. Sometimes I imagined that the fiend had followed me, and he planned to murder my companion to speed the progress of my work. When these thoughts possessed me, I would not leave Henry for a moment and followed him like a shadow, to protect him from the perceived rage of his destroyer. I was haunted by the feeling that I had committed some great crime. While I was not guilty, I had brought a horrible curse down upon myself that was as terrible as a crime.

The city of Edinburgh should have interested even the most unfortunate being, but I looked upon the city with sluggish eyes and mind. The historical aspect of Oxford pleased Clerval more than Edinburgh. But, the beauty and regularity of the new city of Edinburgh, its romantic castle and delightful surroundings, Arthur's Seat, St. Bernard's Well, and the Pentland Hills made up for the change and filled him with pleasure and admiration. But, I was impatient to arrive at my destination.

We left Edinburgh after one week, passing through Coupar, St. Andrew's, and along the banks of the Tay, to Perth, where our friend was expecting us. I was in no mood to laugh and talk with strangers and enter into their feelings and plans with the good humor expected from a guest. Accordingly, I told Clerval that I wanted to travel through Scotland alone. "Enjoy yourself," I said, "and let us meet back here. I might be gone for a month or two. Please do not try to interfere with my plans, I beg you to leave me alone for a short time. When I come back, I hope to feel better, and be better company for you."

Henry wanted to discourage me, but he did not argue when he saw that I was resolved on this plan. He asked me to write to him often. He said, "I would rather be with you in your solitary rambles, than with these Scotch people who are strangers. Hurry and come back, my dear friend, I will not feel at home until you return."

Having left my friend, I decided to travel to some remote spot in Scotland and finish my work in solitude. I did not doubt that the monster followed me, and he would reveal himself to me when I was finished, so that he could welcome his companion. With this plan in mind, I traveled through the northern highlands and chose one of the remote Orkneys as the scene of my labor. It was a fit place for such work, hardly more than a rock with high sides continuously beaten by the waves. The soil was barren. The pasture scarcely supported a few miserable cows, and provided enough oatmeal for the five inhabitants whose miserable diet was evident by their gaunt, scraggy appearance. Luxuries such as bread and vegetables, and even fresh water, had to be brought from the mainland, which was about five miles away.

There were three miserable huts on the whole island. One of the huts was empty when I arrived, and the state of the two rooms reflected extreme poverty. The thatch roof had fallen in, the walls were unplastered, and the door was coming off the hinges. I rented this hut and ordered it to be repaired, bought some furniture, and moved in. My arrival might have surprised the cottagers if they were not numbed by extreme poverty and want. As it happened, nobody bothered me, and I was hardly thanked for the food and clothing I doled out, so much had suffering blunted the people's feelings.

I devoted the mornings to work, but in the evening, when the weather allowed, I walked along the stony beach and listened to the waves as they roared and dashed at my feet. It was a monotonous yet ever-changing scene. I thought about Switzerland, which was very different from this desolate, appalling landscape. The hills of Switzerland are covered with vines, and the cottages are scattered thickly on the plains. The fair lakes reflect the gentle, blue sky, and even when the water is troubled by winds, the tumult does not compare to the roaring of the giant ocean.

I arranged my schedule this way when I first arrived, but as I progressed, the work seemed more horrible and burdensome every day. Sometimes I could not make myself enter my laboratory for several days. At other times, I labored day and night to complete my work. Without a doubt, I was engaged in a filthy process. During my first experiment, a kind of enthusiastic frenzy had blinded me to the horror of my actions. My mind was fixed intently on the outcome of my project, and I had shut my eyes to the horror of my proceedings. But, now that I was acting in cold blood, my heart was often sickened by the work of my hands.

Living this way, engaged in the most horrible work, immersed in solitude with nothing to distract my attention from the actual surroundings, my mood became unstable. I grew nervous and restless. Every minute, I feared to see my persecutor. Sometimes I sat staring at the ground, afraid to raise my eyes in case I should see the being I dreaded to see. I was afraid to leave the sight of my fellow creatures, in case he should find me alone and come to claim his companion.

Meanwhile, I continued to work, and my project was already far advanced. I looked forward to its completion with tremendous, eager hope. I did not trust myself to question this hope, but it was mixed with vague foreboding of evil that made me feel sick at heart.

∞∞∞∞∞∞∞∞∞∞∞∞∞∞∞∞∞∞∞

Chapter 20

One evening I was sitting in my laboratory after the sun had set and the moon was just rising from the sea. I did not have enough light for my work, and I wondered whether I should stop work for the night or keep going so that I could finish my project more quickly. As I sat, I considered what the effects of my project might be. Three years before, I had engaged in the same kind of work and created a fiend whose cruelty desolated my heart and filled it with bitter remorse. I was about to create another being without knowing anything about her nature. She might be ten thousand times more violent than her mate and delight in murder and wretchedness for its own sake. He had promised to live far away from human civilization and hide himself in remote places, but she had not promised. She would likely become a thinking, reasoning animal, and she might not comply with an agreement made before her creation. It was possible they would hate each other. The creature already hated his own deformity. Perhaps he would hate himself even more when he saw his own deformity in female form. She might turn away from him with disgust and prefer the superior beauty of human beings. She might leave him, and he would be alone again. He would experience the fresh aggravation of being deserted by one of his own species. Even if they left Europe and lived in the remote parts of the new world, they might have children and create a race of devils that would terrorize humankind. Did I have the right to inflict this curse on future generations? I had been moved by the arguments of the being I had created. I had been struck senseless by his fiendish threats. For the first time, I considered the wickedness of my promise. I shuddered to think that future generations might consider me their destroyer. They might think I had traded the existence of the whole human race for my own benefit.

136

I shuddered, and my heart failed me. Looking up, I saw the demon standing by the window in the moonlight. A ghastly grin wrinkled his face as he gazed at me, working on the task he had assigned. Yes, he had followed me in my travels. He had wandered through forests, hidden himself in caves, or taken refuge in wide and desolate meadows. Now he had come to check on my progress and claim the fulfillment of my promise.

As I looked at him, his face expressed the utmost malice and treachery. With a feeling of madness, I thought that I had promised to create another being like him. Trembling with passion, I tore the thing I had created to pieces. The wretch saw me destroy the creature he relied on for his future happiness. He withdrew with a howl of devilish revenge and despair.

I locked the door and left the room, vowing never to resume my work. With trembling steps, I returned to my own rooms. I was alone, with nobody nearby to help dispel the gloom and relieve the sickening oppressiveness of my thoughts.

Several hours passed, and I remained near the window, gazing at the sea. The winds were hushed, and the sea was nearly still. All nature rested under the eye of the quiet moon. A few fishing vessels floated on the water, and the gentle breeze carried the voices of the fishermen calling to one another. I was hardly conscious of the profound silence until I heard the sound of oars paddling near the shore and a person landed close to my house.

A few minutes later, I heard the creaking as my door opening softly. I trembled from head to foot. I sensed who had come, and I wanted to call the peasant who lived near my cottage, but I was overcome by helplessness. I felt the way you might feel in a nightmare when danger approaches, and you vainly try to escape, but you are rooted to the spot. I heard the sound of footsteps walking along the hall, then the door opened, and the wretch whom I dreaded appeared.

Shutting the door, he came close to me and said in a low voice, "You have destroyed the work that you began. What do you plan to do? Do you dare to break your promise? I have endured toil and misery. I left Switzerland with you and crept along the shores of the Rhine, among its willowy islands, and over the tops of the hills. I have lived for many months among the meadows of England, and the deserted places of Scotland. I have endured untold fatigue, and cold, and hunger. Do you dare destroy my hopes?"

"Leave here! I do break my promise. I will never create another being as deformed and wicked as yourself."

"Slave! I reasoned with you before. You have proved that you are not worthy of my consideration. Remember that I have power. You think that you are miserable, but I can make you so wretched that the light of day will seem hateful. You are my creator, but I am your master. Obey!"

"I have made my decision. Even though you are powerful, your threats will not make me do this wicked act. I am determined not to create an evil companion for you. Shall I release a demon who delights in wretchedness and death upon the earth? Leave here! My decision is firm, and your words will only make me angry."

The monster saw the determination in my face and gnashed his teeth in futile anger. "Shall every man find a wife," he said, "and every animal have his mate, and I must be alone? My feelings of affection were met with scorn and hatred. Man! You may hate, but beware! You will spend your life in dread and misery. Soon the bolt will fall which destroys your happiness forever. Will you be happy, while I am consumed by unhappiness? You can blast my other feelings, but revenge remains. From this day, revenge will be more important to me than light or food. You are my tyrant and tormentor. I might die, but first you will curse the sun that looks down on your misery. Beware, I fear nothing, and that makes me powerful. I will watch you with the cleverness of a snake, and I will sting with venom. Man, you will regret the harm you do to me."

"Stop, devil, and do not bother me with your evil words. I have told you my decision. I am not a coward to be swayed by your words. Leave me, I will not change my mind."

"I will go, but remember, I will be with you on your wedding night."

I sprang forward and exclaimed, "Villain! Watch out for your own safety, before you threaten me."

I would have seized him, but he eluded my grasp and quickly left the house. A few moments later, I saw his boat shoot across the water like a swift arrow. The boat was soon lost among the waves.

It was silent, but his words rang in my ears. I burned with rage. I wanted to pursue the being who had destroyed my peace. I wanted to throw him into the ocean. I paced back and forth in my room, and pictured a thousand images that tormented me. Why had I not followed and fought him? I had allowed him to leave, and he had gone towards the mainland. I shuddered to think who might be the next victim, sacrificed for his revenge. I remembered his words, "I WILL BE WTH YOU ON YOUR WEDDING NIGHT." I would meet my fate on that day. I would die and satisfy his malice. The thought did not frighten me, but tears streamed from my eyes when I recalled my beloved Elizabeth. I wept for the first time in many months, when I thought about her tears and endless sorrow at having her lover so cruelly taken away. I resolved that I would not accept defeat without bitter struggle.

The night passed away, and the sun rose from the ocean. My feelings changed from violent rage to deep despair. I left the house, which was the scene of last night's horrible confrontation, and walked along the beach. The sea seemed like an insurmountable barrier between me and my fellow creatures. I wished it could truly keep me separate.

I wanted to live out my life on that barren rock. It would be a wearisome life, it is true, but I would not face any misery or sudden shock. If I returned home, I must either be sacrificed myself, or watch the people I loved die at the hands of a demon I had created.

I walked around the island like a restless spirit who was miserable because he was separated from everything he loved. About noon, when the sun had risen high in the sky, I lay down on the grass and fell into a deep sleep. I had stayed awake the whole night. My nerves were agitated, and my eyes were inflamed by watchfulness and misery. When I awoke, I felt refreshed and more like myself, as if I belonged to the human race. I began to think more calmly about what had happened, yet the words of the fiend still rang in my ears. It seemed like a dream, but distinct and oppressive as a reality.

It was late in the afternoon, and I remained on the shore, eating an oatcake to satisfy my hunger. I saw a fishing-boat land close to me, and one of the men brought me a packet. It contained letters from Geneva and one letter from Clerval, begging me to join him. He felt that he was wasting his time in Scotland, and his acquaintances in London wanted him to return so they could finish planning for his India enterprise. He could no longer delay his departure. It was possible that he would leave soon for his journey to India, and he wanted me to spend as much time with him as possible before he left. He asked me to leave my solitary island and meet him at Perth, so that we could travel to London together.

This letter recalled me to life in some degree. I determined to leave the island within two days.

Before I left, I would have to perform one task which I shuddered to consider. In order to pack my chemical instruments, I would have to enter the room which was the scene of my disgusting work. I knew the very sight of the instruments would make me feel sick. The next morning, I summoned my courage and unlocked the door of the laboratory. The remains of the half-finished creature, whom I had destroyed, lay scattered on the floor. I almost felt that I had mangled the living flesh of a human being. I paused to pull myself together before I went into the room. With trembling hands, I carried the instruments out of the room. I reflected that I should not leave the evidence of my work, which would horrify the peasants. I put the remains into a basket, covering them with a great quantity of stones, and determined to throw them into the sea that night. Meanwhile, I sat on the beach, cleaning and organizing my chemical instruments.

My feelings had changed completely since that night the demon had appeared. Before, I had regarded my promise with gloomy despair, as something I must fulfill regardless of the consequences. Now, I felt that I could see clearly for the first time. I did not consider renewing my work for one instant. The threats I had heard weighed on my thoughts, but I would not try to prevent what might happen by making another creature like the fiend. It would be a low and selfish act. I did not allow myself to think otherwise.

Between two and three o'clock in the morning, the moon rose. I sailed about four miles from shore in a small boat, taking my basket. The scene was perfectly solitary. A few boats were returning back towards land, but I sailed away from them. I felt sick with anxiety, as if I was about to commit some terrible crime, and I avoided meeting people.

The sky was clear, but when the moon was suddenly covered by a dark cloud, I took advantage of the moment of darkness and threw the basket into the sea. I listened to the gurgling sound as it sank and sailed away from the spot. The sky became cloudy, but the air was pure, chilled by the rising breeze from the northeast. The wind refreshed me, and I decided to stay out on the water. Fixing the rudder, I lay down in the bottom of the boat. Clouds covered the moon, everything looked hazy, and the only sound I heard was the boat cutting through the water. I was lulled by the murmuring sound, and within a short time I fell into a sound sleep.

I do not know how long I slept, but when I awoke the sun had risen, and it was already late in the morning. The wind was high, and the waves threatened the safety of my small boat. The wind had driven me far from the coast I had left. I tried to change my course, but quickly found that my boat filled with water every time I made the attempt. My only option was to let the wind drive me forward. I confess that I felt terrified by my situation. I had no compass. I could not use the sun as a guide since I knew little about the geography of this part of the world. I might be driven out into the wide Atlantic and face the tortures of starvation, or I might be swallowed up by the immeasurable, roaring waters that buffeted my boat. I had already been out for many hours and felt the torment of burning thirst, which was prelude to the further suffering I would face. I looked at the sky, covered by quickly-moving clouds that flew before the wind. I looked upon the sea which would be my grave. "Fiend!" I exclaimed. "Your task is already fulfilled." I thought about Elizabeth, and my father, and Clerval – all left behind and subject to the monster's merciless passions. This idea filled me with such frightful despair that I shudder to remember, even now when I am close to leaving this world forever.

Some hours passed this way. As the sun declined towards the horizon, the wind died down to a gentle breeze, and the sea became free of breakers. The breakers gave way to a heavy swell. I was feeling sick and hardly able to hold the rudder, when I saw a line of high land towards the south.

Even though I was utterly exhausted by fatigue and the dreadful suspense I had endured for several hours, this sudden certainty of life rushed like a flood of warm joy to my heart. Tears gushed from my eyes.

Our feelings change so quickly. It is strange how we cling to life even when we are overcome by misery! I used part of my clothing to make another sail, and eagerly set a course towards the land. It looked rocky and wild, but as I came closer I could easily see traces of cultivation. I saw vessels near the shore and found myself suddenly transported back to civilization. I followed the winding shoreline carefully, sailing in the direction of a steeple I saw rising from behind a cliff. I felt extremely weak and decided to sail directly towards the town, where I could find something to eat. Fortunately, I had carried some money with me.

As I turned the bend, I saw a small, neat town with a good harbor. Entering the harbor, I felt my heart bounding with joy at my unexpected escape.

I was busy fixing the boat and arranging the sails, when I saw several people crowding towards me. They seemed surprised by my appearance. Instead of offering me any help, they stood whispering together with gestures that might have alarmed me at any other time. I observed that they spoke English and addressed them in that language. "My good friends," I said, "Could you tell me where I am, and the name of this town?"

"You will know that soon enough," replied a man with a hoarse voice. "Maybe you have come to a place you will not like very much. You will have no choice about your living quarters, I promise you."

I was surprised to receive such a rude answer from a stranger, and I was startled to see the frowning, angry faces of his companions. "Why do you answer me so rudely?" I replied. "Surely, it is not the custom of Englishmen to greet strangers in such a rude way."

"I do not know what the custom of the English may be," the man said, "but it is the custom of the Irish to hate villains." While this strange conversation continued, I saw the crowd increase rapidly. The people's faces expressed a mixture of curiosity and anger, which both annoyed and alarmed me to some degree.

I asked directions to the inn, but nobody replied. When I moved forward, a murmuring sound rose from the crowd as they followed and surrounded me. A disagreeable-looking man tapped me on the shoulder and said, "Come on, you must follow me to Mr. Kirwin's to explain what you are doing here."

"Who is Mr. Kirwin? Why do I have to explain myself? Is this not a free country?"

"Yes, sir, it is free enough for honest folks. Mr. Kirwin is a magistrate, and you must tell him what you know about the death of a gentleman who was found murdered here last night."

This answer startled me, but I tried to stay calm. I could easily prove that I was innocent. I followed the man silently, and he led me to one of the best houses in the town. I was almost fainting from hunger and fatigue, but I roused all my strength, giving the crowd no opportunity to confuse signs of physical weakness with guilt. Little did I expect the calamity that would soon overwhelm me, and replace all fear of shame or death with horror and despair. I must pause here, for it takes all my strength to recall the frightful events I am about to describe.

Chapter 21

I was soon brought before the magistrate, who was a kind, old man with calm, mild manners. He looked at me with some degree of severity, and then turned toward the men who had brought me and asked who would serve as witnesses in this instance.

The magistrate chose one man from the half dozen who came forward. The man stated that he had been out fishing with his son and his brother-in-law, Daniel Nugent, the night before. About ten o'clock, they noticed a strong northerly blast rising, and they headed for port. It was a very dark night, since the moon had not yet risen. They landed at a creek two miles below the harbor. The man walked ahead, carrying part of the fishing tackle, and his companions followed behind.

As he walked along the sands, his foot struck something, and he fell face forward on the ground. His companions came to help him, and by the light of their lantern they found that he had fallen on the body of a man who appeared to be dead. At first, they guessed the man must have drowned and washed up on shore. But, examining the man, they found the clothes were not wet, and he was not yet cold. They quickly carried the body to the cottage of an old woman who lived nearby and tried in vain to revive him to life. He seemed to be a handsome young man about twenty-five years old. It seemed he had been strangled, because he was unhurt except for the black mark of fingers around his neck.

The first part of the witness statement did not interest me, but when he described the mark of fingers, I recalled the murder of my brother and began to grow agitated. My arms and legs trembled, and my sight became blurred. I had to lean on a chair for support. The magistrate watched me sharply, and of course he thought I appeared guilty.

The son confirmed his father's story. When Daniel Nugent was called, he swore positively that just before his companion fell, he saw a boat carrying a single man a short distance from shore. As far as he could judge from the starlight, it was the same boat that I had just landed. A woman testified that she lived near the beach, and she had been standing in the doorway of her cottage, waiting for the fishermen to return, about an hour before the body was discovered. She had seen a boat carrying one man pushing off from the part of the shore where the body was later found.

Another woman confirmed that the fishermen had brought the body to her house. It was not cold, and they had put the man into bed, and rubbed his body. Daniel went to town to bring back an apothecary, but the man's life was quite gone.

Several other men were questioned, and they agreed that the strong north wind must have beaten against my boat for several hours and forced me to return to the same place I had left. Besides, it appeared that I had brought the body from another place, and I did not seem to know the shore. I might have landed at the harbor without knowing how far the town of --- ----- might be from the place I had left the body.

After hearing this evidence, Mr. Kirwin decided I should be taken to see the body. He wanted to observe how I would respond. My extreme agitation when the murder was described might have suggested this idea. The magistrate, and several other people, conducted me to the inn. I could not help being struck by the strange coincidences that had taken place during this eventful night. I was not worried, knowing that I had spoken to several people on the island at the same time the murder was committed. I entered the room where the body lay and was led to the coffin. How can I describe my feelings when I saw it? I feel horrified even now, and I cannot recall that terrible moment without shuddering in agony. I forgot the inquiry, and the presence of the magistrate and witnesses, when I saw the lifeless

146

form of Henry Clerval stretched in front of me. I gasped for breath and threw myself on the body. "My dearest Henry," I exclaimed, "Have my murderous actions taken your life? I have already destroyed two lives, and other victims await their destiny, but you, Clerval, my friend, my benefactor – "

My human frame could no longer support the agony I endured, and I was carried out of the room suffering convulsions. I developed a fever and lay for two months on the brink of death. I heard afterward that my ravings were frightful. I called myself the murderer of William, Justine, and Clerval. Sometimes I begged my caretakers to help me destroy the fiend who tormented me. At other times, I felt the monster's fingers already grasping my neck and screamed out loud with agony and terror. Fortunately, I spoke in my native language, and Mr. Kirwin was the only person who understood me, but my gestures and bitter cries were enough to frighten the other witnesses. Why didn't I die? I was more miserable than any man before. Why didn't I sink into forgetfulness and rest? Death takes many blooming children away from their loving parents. How many brides and youthful lovers are alive and hopeful one day, and the next day they are decaying in the tomb? How could I stand the constant torture?

But, I was doomed to live, and two months later I awoke, as if from a dream, and found myself in prison. I was stretched on a wretched bed, surrounded by jailers, guards, bolts, and all the miserable trappings of a dungeon. I remember it was morning when I regained consciousness. I had forgotten the details of what had happened, and only felt that some great misfortune had overwhelmed me. When I looked around and saw the barred windows and the squalid room, I remembered everything and groaned bitterly.

This sound disturbed an old woman who was sleeping on the chair beside me. She was a hired nurse, the wife of one of the jailers, and her face expressed the worst qualities of her class.

Her expression was hard and rude, and she looked like someone who was used to seeing people suffer without feeling sympathy. Her tone expressed her complete indifference. She spoke to me in English, and I recalled hearing her voice during my sufferings. "Are you better now, sir?" she said.

I replied in the same language, saying weakly, "I think I am. If it is all true, and not a dream, I am sorry that I am still alive to feel this misery and horror."

"If you mean about the gentleman you murdered," the old woman replied, "I think it might be better if you were dead. I fancy it will go hard with you! But, that's none of my business. I am sent to nurse you and get you well. I do my duty with a clear conscience. It would be good if everybody did the same."

I turned with loathing from this woman who could speak so unkindly to a person just saved from the brink of death. But, I felt exhausted and unable to reflect on everything that had happened. The events of my life seemed like a dream. I sometimes doubted that it was all true, since my memories did not have the force of reality.

As the floating images in my mind became more distinct, I grew feverish and darkness pressed around me. No kind person was near to soothe me with gentle words, and no loving hand supported me. The doctor came and prescribed medicines for me, and the old woman prepared them. The doctor seemed utterly careless, and the old woman's face expressed brutality. Who could be interested in the fate of a murderer except the hangman who would gain his fee?

These were my first thoughts, but I soon learned that Mr. Kirwin had shown me extreme kindness. He had given me the best room in the prison, wretched as it was, and he had provided the doctor and nurse. It is true that he seldom came to see me. While he wanted to relieve the suffering of every human creature, he did not want to listen to the agony and miserable ravings of a murderer. He came to make certain that I was not

148

neglected, but his visits were short and infrequent. One day, while I gradually recovering, I sat in a chair with my eyes half open and my cheeks pale as death. I was overcome by misery and gloom, and I often reflected that it would be better to seek death than remain in a world which seemed so wretched to me. At one time, I considered whether I should declare myself guilty and suffer the penalty of law. I was less innocent than poor Justine. I was thinking about these things when the door of my room opened, and Mr. Kirwin entered. His face expressed sympathy and kindness. He pulled a chair close to mine and spoke to me in French. "I am afraid this place is very shocking to you," he said. "Can I do anything to make you more comfortable?"

"I thank you, but nothing in this world can comfort me."

"I know the sympathy of a stranger can give little relief when you are oppressed by such strange misfortune. But, I hope you will soon leave this unhappy place. Surely, evidence can be brought forward to free you from the criminal charge."

"That is the least of my concerns. Through a series of strange events, I have become the most miserable of human beings. I have been, and continue to be, persecuted and tortured. Can death seem evil to me?"

"Nothing can be more unfortunate and agonizing than the recent events. This shore is renowned for its hospitality. You were thrown on this shore by some accident, seized immediately, and charged with murder. The first sight that was presented to you was the body of your friend, murdered in such a strange way, and placed in your path, as if by some fiend."

I felt agitated as Mr. Kirwin described my sufferings, but I also felt surprised by how much he seemed to know about me. I must have appeared astonished, because Mr. Kirwin quickly added, "When you first became ill, your papers were brought to me. I examined them, looking for some address so I could notify your relatives about your misfortune and illness. I found several letters, including one from your father. I wrote to Geneva right away, and nearly two months have passed since I sent the letter. But, you are ill, you tremble, you are still not ready for any kind of excitement."

"The suspense is a thousand times worse than the most terrible event. Tell me, what new death has happened? What murder must I grieve now?"

"Your family is perfectly well," Mr. Kirwin said gently, "and someone, a friend, has come to visit you."

I don't know what put the idea into my mind, but I instantly thought the murderer must have come to taunt me, and mock me in my misery. He would use Clerval's death to make me comply with his hellish desires. I put my hand in front of my eyes and cried out in agony, "Oh! Take him away! I can't see him, for God's sake, don't let him come."

Mr. Kirwin looked at me with a troubled expression. He could not help thinking my outburst was a sign of guilt. He said in a rather severe tone, "Young man, I should have thought you would be pleased to see your father, instead of reacting so violently against it."

"My father!" I cried, and every fiber of my being relaxed from anguish to happiness. "Has my father really come? How kind, how very kind! But, where is he? Why doesn't he come see me?"

The change in my manner surprised and pleased the magistrate. Perhaps he thought my earlier outburst was a momentary return of delirium. Now he resumed his former kind manner. Rising, he left the room with my nurse, and after a minute my father entered.

Nothing could have given me greater pleasure at that moment than the arrival of my father. I stretched out my hand to him and said, "Are you safe – and Elizabeth – and Ernest?" My father reassured me that they were well. He tried to raise my despondent spirits by talking about my family and the subjects close to my heart. But, he soon realized that a prison is not a cheerful place.

"My son, what a place this is!" he said, looking mournfully at the barred windows and the wretched appearance of the room. You traveled to look for happiness, and fatality seems to pursue you. And poor Clerval – "

The name of my unfortunate, murdered friend made me more agitated than I could bear in my weakened state. I wept and said, "Alas! Yes, father, some horrible destiny hangs over me. I will have to live to fulfill it, or I surely would have died on Henry's coffin."

We were not allowed to talk for long. The fragile state of my health required that I should remain calm. Mr. Kriwin came in and insisted that my strength should not be exhausted by too much excitement. But, I felt that my father was like my good angel. Gradually, I recovered my health.

As my sickness diminished, I was absorbed by gloomy, black depression that noting could lift. I constantly pictured the ghastly, murdered image of Clerval. More than once, my thoughts made me so agitated my friends feared I might have a dangerous relapse. Alas! Why did they save such a hated, miserable life? It was certain that I must fulfill my destiny, which was coming closer. Soon, very soon, death will extinguish this throbbing and relieve me from this burden of anguish that crushes me to the dust. Justice will be fulfilled, and I will sink into rest. At that time, death still seemed distant, although I frequently wished to die. I often sat for hours without moving or speaking, wishing that some mighty calamity would consume both me and my destroyer.

The time for the court trial approached. I had already been in prison for three months. I was still weak, and constantly in danger of relapse, but I was forced to travel nearly one hundred miles to the country town where the court was held. Mr. Kirwin took great care in collecting witnesses and arranging my defense. I was spared the disgrace of appearing publicly as a criminal since the case was not brought before the court. The grand jury rejected the case when it was proved that I was on the Orkney Islands at the time my friend's body was found. Two weeks after we arrived in the town, I was released from prison.

My father was overjoyed when I was freed from the criminal charge. I could breathe the fresh air again, and I was allowed to return to my native country. I did not share his feelings, since the walls of a dungeon or a palace seemed equally hateful to me. The cup of life was poisoned forever. The sun shone down on me, just as it did on those who were happy and light-hearted, but I saw only dense, frightful darkness. No light could penetrate the darkness, but the glimmer of two eyes glared upon me. Sometimes they were the expressive eyes of Henry, languishing in death, his dark eyes nearly closed, fringed with long, black lashes. Sometimes I saw the watery, clouded eyes of the monster as I first saw them in my room at Ingolstadt.

My father tried to awaken the feelings of affection within me. He talked about Elizabeth and Ernest, and he talked about Geneva, which I would soon visit. His words only drew deep groans from me. Sometimes I did wish for happiness. I thought about my beloved cousin with melancholy delight, and longed to see once more the blue lake I had loved as a child. My usual state of feeling was indifference. Divine nature seemed no different to me than a prison. My indifference was interrupted only by spasms of anguish and despair. At these moments, I tried to end the life I hated so much, and it required constant, careful vigilance to restrain me from committing some dreadful act of violence.

One duty still remained to me, and it finally triumphed over my despair. I must return to Geneva without delay so that I could watch over the lives of the people I loved, and wait for the murderer. If I happened to find his hiding place, or he dared to visit me again, I would take unfailing aim and destroy the monstrous form I had imbued with an even more monstrous soul. My father wanted to delay our departure, since he was afraid the journey might be too strenuous for me. I was a shattered wreck, the shadow of a human being. My strength was gone. I was a mere skeleton, and fever preyed upon my wasted form day and night. Still, I was so impatient to leave Ireland, my father thought it best to agree. We took passage on a vessel bound for Havre-de-Grace, and sailed with a fair wind from the Irish shore. It was midnight, and I lay on the deck looking at the stars and listening to the dashing of the waves. I welcomed the darkness that shut Ireland from my sight. My pulse beat with feverish joy when I reflected that I would soon see Geneva again. The past seemed like a fearful dream,, but the ship, and the wind that blew me from the hated shore of Ireland, and the sea that surrounded me, told me forcibly that it was not a dream. My dearest friend and companion Clerval had fallen victim to me, and the monster I had created. I recalled the memories of my whole life, my quiet happiness living with my family in Geneva, my mother's death, my departure for Ingolstadt. I shuddered when I recalled the mad enthusiasm that hurried me toward the creation of my hideous enemy. I remembered the night when he first lived. I could not continue with my thoughts. A thousand feelings pressed upon me, and I wept bitterly. Ever since I had recovered from the fever, it had become my habit to take a small amount of laudanum every night. It was the only way I could sleep, and get enough rest to allow me to live. Oppressed by my memories, I now swallowed double my usual dose and fell into deep sleep. But, sleep did not bring e respite from thought and misery. My dreams presented a thousand images that frightened me. Towards morning I was possessed by a nightmare. I felt the fiend's grasp on my neck, and I could not free myself from it. My ears rang with groans and cries. My father was watching over me, and he noticed my restlessness. He woke me, and I saw the cloudy sky above and the dashing waves around. The fiend was not here. I felt a sense of security as if some kind of truce had been established between the present moment and the irresistible, disastrous future. The human mind is strangely susceptible to this kind of calm forgetfulness.

ᐯᐯᐯᐯᐯᐯᐯᐯᐯᐯᐯᐯᐯᐯᐯᐯᐯ

Chapter 22

The voyage came to an end. We landed and traveled to Paris. I soon found that I had overtaxed my strength. I had to rest before I could continue my journey. My father's care and attention were tireless, but he did not know the real cause of my suffering. He tried mistaken methods to remedy something that could not be cured. He wanted me to seek amusement in society, when I hated the sight of human beings. Oh, I did not hate them! They were my brothers, my fellow beings, and I was attracted to even the most repulsive among them. They seemed like heavenly creatures with angelic nature. But, I felt that I had no right to share their society. I had unchained an enemy among them who found joy in shedding their blood and hearing their groans. Every one of them would hate me, and hunt me from the world, if they knew about my unhallowed acts and the crimes I had caused to happen!

My father finally accepted my desire to avoid society, and he tried various arguments to banish my despair. Sometimes, he thought I felt ashamed because I had been accused of murder. He tried to tell me it was useless to hold on to pride.

"Alas!" I said. "You know me very little, father. It would be degrading to human feeling if somebody as wretched as I felt pride. Poor, unhappy Justine. Justine was innocent, she faced the same charge, and she died for it. I was the cause – I murdered her. William, Justine, Henry – they all died because of me."

My father had often heard me accuse myself during my imprisonment. He sometimes wished to know the explanation. At other times, he thought it must be related to my delirium. He thought I had imagined something of this kind during my illness, and I still retained the idea now that my health was improving.

I avoided explanation, and maintained complete silence about the wretch I had created. I was convinced that I would be considered insane. This belief was enough to keep me silent forever. Besides, I could not bring myself to disclose a secret that would shock my father and fill his heart with horror and fear. I restrained my impatient desire for sympathy, and kept silent when I would have given the world to confide the fatal secret. Still, I could not control the self-accusation that burst from me at times. I could not explain my words, but speaking the truth helped relieve the burden of my misery. On this occasion, my father said with surprise, "My dearest Victor, why are you obsessed with this idea? My dear son, I beg you never to say such things again."

"I am not crazy," I cried energetically. "The sun and the sky know my actions, they can bear witness to my truth. I have murdered those innocent victims. They died because of my actions. I would have shed my own blood, drop by drop, to save them. But, I could not save them, Father, I could not sacrifice the whole human race."

The final part of this speech convinced my father that my thoughts were deranged. He instantly changed the subject of our conversation, and tried to change the course of my thoughts. He wanted me to forget what had happened in Ireland, and he never talked about it, or allowed me to talk about my misfortunes there.

I became calmer as time passed. I was still miserable, but I did not talk about my crimes in the same incoherent way. It was enough that I was conscious of them. I forced myself to curb the imperious voice of wretchedness that wanted to declare itself to the whole world. Outwardly, I appeared more calm and composed than I had been since my journey to the sea of ice. A few days before we left Paris to return to Switzerland, I received the following letter from Elizabeth:

"My dear Friend,

It gave me the greatest pleasure to receive a letter from my uncle addressed from Paris. You no longer seem so far away. I am hoping to see you in two weeks. My poor cousin, how much you must have suffered! I expect you are more ill now than you were when you left Geneva. I have spent a miserable winter, tortured by anxious suspense, but I hope to see peace in your face. I hope to find that your heart is not completely bereft of comfort and tranquility.

Yet, I am afraid the same feelings exist that made you so miserable a year ago. Maybe your unhappy feelings have even increased with time. I do not want to disturb you, when so many misfortunes weigh on you, but I must tell you about a conversation I had with my uncle before he left. It is possible you will say, 'What can Elizabeth have to tell me?' If you really say this, my questions are answered and all my doubts are satisfied. But, you are far from me, and it is possible you may dread, but feel relieved, by what I will say. In case you feel this way, I cannot wait any longer to write to you. I have often wanted to say this to you, but never had the courage to begin.

Victor, you know that your parents have wished for our marriage since we were children. We were brought up to expect this marriage as something which would certainly happen. We were fond of each other as children, and I believe we were close friends as we grew older. But, perhaps we feel the close affection of brother and sister? Tell me, dearest Victor. I beg you to consider our future happiness and tell me the simple truth - Do you love somebody else?

You have traveled, and you have spent several years of your life living at Ingolstadt. I confess to you, my friend, that when I saw you last autumn, so unhappy, preferring solitude to the company of others, I could not help thinking you might regret our relationship. I thought you might feel yourself bound by honor to fulfill the wishes of your parents against your will. But, you should not feel this way. I confess to you, my friend, that I love you. When I dream about the future, you are always my constant friend and companion. But, I want you to be happy as well as myself. Our marriage would make me eternally unhappy if it was not your free choice. You have been crushed by the cruelest misfortunes. It makes me weep to think that you might me denying yourself all hope of love and happiness, which could restore you to yourself, for the sake of 'honor.' My love for you is selfless, but I might be increasing your misery tenfold by being the obstacle to your wishes. Ah, Victor! Please believe that your cousin and playmate loves you sincerely, and this thought makes me miserable. Be happy, my friend. As long as you are happy, be assured that no power on earth can make me unhappy.

Do not let this letter disturb you. Do not answer tomorrow, or the next day, or even until you come, if it gives you pain. My uncle will send me news about your health. If I see one smile on your lips when we meet, I will need no other happiness.

Elizabeth Lavenza
Geneva, May 18th, 17--"

This letter reminded me of the fiend's threat, which I had forgotten - "I WILL BE WITH YOU ON YOUR WEDDING NIGHT!" Such was my punishment. On that night, the demon would use all his powers to destroy me, and tear me away from the glimpse of happiness that might console my suffering. On that night, he had determined to consummate his crimes by killing me. Well, so be it. A deadly struggle would certainly take place. If he was victorious, I would be at peace. If he was vanquished, his power over me would end. I would be a free man. Alas! What freedom? It would be the kind of freedom a peasant enjoys when his family is killed before his eyes, his cottage burned, his lands destroyed, and he is set loose, homeless, penniless, and alone, but free. Such would be my freedom, except that my Elizabeth was a treasure, which would be balanced by the horrors of remorse and guilt that would pursue me until death.

Sweet, beloved Elizabeth! I read and reread her letter. Feelings of love stole into my heart and dared to whisper dreams of paradise and joy. But, the apple was already eaten, and the angel's arm was bared to drive me from all hope. Yet, I would die to make her happy. If the monster carried out his threat, I would die. I considered whether my marriage would hurry my fate. My destruction might arrive a few months sooner. But, if my torturer suspected that I delayed my marriage due to his threat, he would surely find other, perhaps more dreadful, ways to take revenge.

He had vowed TO BE WITH ME ON MY WEDDING NIGHT. But, he did not seem to consider that threat as binding him to peace in the meantime. He had murdered Clerval immediately after making the threat, as if to show me he had not yet satisfied his appetite for killing. I resolved that my enemy's threat would not delay my marriage by a single hour, if my immediate marriage could bring happiness to either Elizabeth or my father.

In this state of mind, I wrote a letter to Elizabeth. My letter was calm and affectionate. "My beloved girl," I said, "I fear that little happiness remains for us on earth. But, all the happiness I might enjoy someday is centered in you. Chase away your fears. To you alone, I consecrate my life and my efforts to be happy. I have one secret Elizabeth, a dreadful one. It will chill you, and horrify you, when it is revealed. Far from being surprised at my misery, you will only wonder that I survived what I had to endure. I will tell you this tale of misery and terror the day after our marriage takes place, because, my sweet cousin, we must have no secrets between us. But, I beg you not to mention it before then. I must request this from you, and I know you will agree."

159

We returned to Geneva about a week after I had received Elizabeth's letter. The sweet girl welcomed me with warm affection, but her eyes filled with tears when she saw my feverish cheeks and my emaciated frame. I saw that she had changed as well. She was thinner, and she had lost much of that heavenly spirit that had charmed me before. But, her gentleness and soft looks of compassion made her better suited to be the companion of someone as blasted and miserable as I was. The momentary peace that I enjoyed did not last. Memory brought madness with it. Real insanity possessed me when I thought about what had happened. Sometimes I was furious and burned with rage, sometimes I was low and despondent. I did not speak or look at anyone, but sat motionless, bewildered by the misery that overwhelmed me.

Elizabeth alone had the power to bring me out of these fits. Her gentle voice would soothe me when I was carried away by passion. She inspired me with human feelings when I sank into torpor. She wept with me and for me. When I was rational, she would argue and encourage acceptance. Ah! Acceptance might be good for those who suffer, but there is no peace for the guilty. The agony of remorse poisons whatever comfort might be found in the expression of grief. Soon after my arrival, my father spoke about my immediate marriage to Elizabeth. I remained silent.

"Do you have some other attachment?"

"None on earth. I love Elizabeth, and look forward to our marriage. Let the day be fixed, and I will consecrate myself, in life or death, to the happiness of my cousin."

"Dear Victor, do not speak this way. We have suffered heavy misfortunes, but let us cling closer to the family who remains. Let us transfer our love for the ones we have lost to the ones who live. Our circle will be small, but we will be bound close by the ties of affection and shared misfortune. When time has softened your despair, new and dear objects of care will be born to replace the ones who were cruelly taken away."

This was my father's message. But, it reminded me of the monster's threat. He seemed so all-powerful in his murderous deeds, you cannot wonder that I regarded him as nearly invincible. When he pronounced the words "I SHALL BE WITH YOU ON YOUR WEDDING NIGHT" I regarded my fate as certain. But, I did not fear death, compared with losing Elizabeth. I assumed a content and cheerful expression and agreed with my father. If my cousin would consent, the ceremony would take place in ten days. I imagined that I had put the seal on my fate.

Great God! If I had guessed the fiend's intention I would have banished myself from my native country and wandered as a friendless outcast over the earth, rather than consent to this miserable marriage. But, the monster seemed to possess magic powers. He had blinded me to his real intention. By preparing for my own death, I hastened the death of a far more beloved victim.

Perhaps from cowardice, or presentiment about the future, I felt my heart sicken within me as the date of our marriage approached. But, I concealed my feelings and pretended to be joyful. My assumed happiness brought smiles to my father's face, but I could not deceive the ever-watchful, observant eye of Elizabeth. She looked forward to our marriage with tranquil contentment, which was mixed with a little fear. Past events had proved that seemingly certain happiness might evaporate and leave nothing behind but deep, everlasting regret. Preparations were made for the event. People came to congratulate us, and everybody was smiling. As well as I could, I concealed my anxiety within my own heart. I entered into my father's plans with enthusiasm, though I knew we might only be preparing for a tragedy. Through my father's efforts, the Austrian government had restored part of Elizabeth's inheritance.

She owned a small property on the shores of Como. We agreed that immediately after our marriage, we would go to the Villa Lavenza and spend our first days of happiness beside the beautiful lake.

In the meantime, I took every precaution to defend myself in case the fiend should attack me openly. I carried pistols and a dagger, and I remained on watch constantly. These efforts gave me a greater feeling of peace. Indeed, as the day approached, the threat seemed more like a delusion, not worth worrying about. At the same time, the happiness I hoped for in my marriage seemed more certain. I heard everyone talking about the marriage as something that no accident could possibly prevent.

Elizabeth seemed happy. My tranquil manner helped to relieve her mind. But, on the day that would fulfill my wishes and my destiny, she was depressed, and she seemed to anticipate some evil. Perhaps she was thinking about the dreadful secret I had promised to share with her the following day. My father was joyful, and busy with preparations, and he mistook his niece's unhappiness for the subdued expression of a bride.

After the ceremony, a large party assembled at my father's house. It was agreed that Elizabeth and I would travel by water, staying at Evian that night, and continuing our voyage the next day. The day was fair, and the wind was favorable. Everyone smiled upon us as we embarked.

Those were the last happy moments of my life. We traveled quickly, the sun was hot, and we took shelter beneath a canopy as we enjoyed the beauty of the scene. Sometimes we traveled along one side of the lake, where we saw Mont Saleve, the pleasant banks of Montalegre, and Mont Blanc towering in the distance, surrounded by snowy mountains. Sometimes we coasted along the opposite coast and saw the mighty Jura presenting a dark, impenetrable wall.

I took Elizabeth's hand. "You are unhappy, my love. Ah! If you knew what I have suffered, what I still might suffer, you would help me enjoy the quiet and freedom of this day."

"Be happy, my dear Victor," Elizabeth replied. "I hope there is nothing to distress you. Be assured that my heart is content, even if I do not appear joyful. Something tells me not to trust the prospect of happiness before us, but I will not listen to such a sinister voice. See how quickly we move along, and how the clouds make the scene even more beautiful. Sometimes the clouds cover Mont Blanc, and sometimes they rise higher. Look at all the fish swimming in the water. The water is so clear we can see every pebble that lies at the bottom. What a divine day! How happy and serene all nature appears!"

Thus Elizabeth tried to distract herself, and me, from all reflection about unhappy subjects. But, her mood varied. Momentary joy shone in her eyes, but it was often replaced by distraction and thoughtfulness.

The sun sank lower in the sky. We passed the river Drance, and observed its path winding through chasms and valleys. We approached the circle of mountains that forms the eastern boundary of the lake. The spire of Evian was surrounded by woods and overhung by range upon range of mountains.

The wind had carried us along with amazing quickness, but now at sunset it sank into a light breeze. The soft air just ruffled the water and caused a pleasant motion among the trees. As we approached the shore, the breeze wafted the most pleasant scent of flowers and hay. The sun sank beneath the horizon as we landed. As I touched the shore, I felt the worries and fears revive which would soon clasp and cling to me forever.

∞∞∞∞∞∞∞∞∞∞∞∞∞∞∞∞∞∞∞∞

Chapter 23

It was eight o'clock when we landed. We walked on the shore for a short time, enjoying the fading light. Afterward we retired to the inn and contemplated the lovely scene of waters, woods and the black outlines of the mountains, obscured ty the darkness but still visible.

The wind, which had fallen in the south, now rose with great violence in the west. The moon had reached its highest point in the sky and was beginning to decline. The clouds swept across the sky, swifter than the flight of vultures, and dimmed the moonlight. The lake reflected the busy scene in the sky, and made it seem even busier with the restless waves that were beginning to rise. Suddenly, a heavy rainstorm descended.

I had been calm during the day, but a thousand fears arose in my mind as soon as night came and darkness obscured the things around me. I was anxious and watchful, and my right hand grasped a pistol which was hidden in my clothes. Every sound terrified me, but I was resolved to fight. I would not shrink from the conflict until my life, or my enemy's life, was extinguished. Elizabeth observed my agitation for some time in timid, fearful silence. Something in my expression frightened her, and she asked, trembling,
"Why are you agitated, my dear Victor? What do you fear?"

"Oh! Peace, peace my love," I replied. "After this night, all will be safe. But, this night is dreadful, very dreadful."

I passed an hour in this state of mind, when it occurred to me that the struggle, which I expected any moment, would be fearful for my wife to witness. I earnestly requested her to retire, and resolved not to join her until I knew where my enemy might be.

She left me, and I continued for some time pacing up and down the passages of the house, inspecting every corner that might provide a hiding place for my adversary. But, I found no

164

trace of him. I was beginning to hope that some fortunate chance had prevented the execution of his threat, when suddenly I heart a shrill and dreadful scream. It came from the room where Elizabeth was sleeping. As I heard it, the whole truth rushed into my mind. For an instant, I felt as if I was frozen in place. My arms dropped, and I could feel the blood flowing through my veins and tingling in my hands and feet. The scream was repeated, and I rushed into the room. Great God! Why did I not die at that moment? Why am I here to describe the destruction of the best hope and the purest creature on earth? She was there, lifeless and unmoving, thrown across the bed, her head hanging down and her pale, distorted features half covered by her hair. Everywhere I turn, I see the same image – her bloodless arms and limp figure flung by the murderer on her bridal bed. Could I behold this and live? Alas! Life is stubborn and clings most closely where it is most hated. I lost consciousness and fell to the ground.

When I recovered, I found myself surrounded by the people of the inn. Their faces expressed breathless horror, but the horror of others seemed to be a mockery, a shadow, of the feelings that oppressed me. I escaped from them to the room where the body of Elizabeth lay, my love, my wife, so recently alive, so dear, so worthy. She had been moved from the position where I first saw her, and now she lay with her head leaning against her arm, with a handkerchief covering her face and neck. She might have been asleep. I rushed towards her and embraced her passionately. The deadly stillness and coldness of her limbs told me that the form I held in my arms was no longer the Elizabeth I had loved and cherished. The murderous mark of the fiend's grasp was on her neck, and the breath had ceased to flow from her lips. While I still hung over her, in the agony of despair, I happened to look up. The windows of the room had been dark earlier, and I felt a kind of panic when I saw the yellow light of the moon illuminate the chamber. The shutters had been thrown back, and I saw, with horror that cannot be described, a hideous, detested figure. A grin was on the monster's face and he seemed to jeer, as he pointed towards the corpse of my wife with his fiendish finger. I rushed towards the window. I fired, pulling the pistol from my shirt, but he eluded me. Leaping from his place, and running with the swiftness of lighting, he plunged into the lake.

The noise of the pistol brought a crowd of people into the room. I pointed to the spot where he had disappeared, and we followed the track with boats. Nets were cast, but without result. We returned, hopeless, after several hours, and most of my companions believed I had imagined the form. After landing, they searched through the countryside, with parties going in different directions through the woods and vines.

I tried to go with them, and proceeded a short distance from the house, when I became dizzy and my steps faltered like a drunken man. I fell at last into a state of utter exhaustion, darkness covered my eyes, and I became feverish. In this state, I was carried back and placed on a bed, hardly conscious of what had happened. My eyes wandered around the room as if I was looking for something I had lost.

After some time, I arose and crawled, as if by instinct, towards the room where the corpse of my beloved lay. There were women around the bed weeping. I hung over the body, and my sad tears mingled with their tears. All this time, my thoughts were confused, as I recalled my misfortunes and their cause. I thought about the death of William, the execution of Justine, the murder of Clerval, and finally my wife. Even at that moment, I could not be sure that my remaining family was safe from the evil intentions of the fiend. Even now, my father might be writhing under his grasp, and Ernest might be dead at his feet. This thought made me shudder, and recalled me to action. I jumped up and resolved to return to Geneva as quickly as I could.

There was no way to get horses, so I must return by the lake. The wind was against me, and the rain fell in torrents. But, it was hardly morning, and I could hope to arrive by night. I hired men to row, and took an oar myself, because I had always found relief from mental torment in bodily exercise. But, the overflowing misery I now felt, and the extreme agitation I had suffered, made me incapable of any exertion. I threw down my oar, leaned my head on my hands, and gave way to every gloomy thought that arose. When I looked up, I saw scenes that were familiar to me in happier moments. I had contemplated those scenes just the day before with Elizabeth who was now a shadow and a memory. Tears streamed from my eyes. The rain had stopped for the moment, and I saw the fish playing in the waters as they had done a few hours before when Elizabeth watched them. Nothing is as painful to the human mind as a great and sudden change. The sun might shine, or the clouds might threaten, but nothing could appear to me the way it had the day before. A fiend had snatched from me every hope of human happiness. No creature had ever been as miserable as I was. My frightful experience was unique in human history. But, why should I dwell on the incidents that followed this final overwhelming event? My story has been full of horrors. I have reached their summit, and I what I must now describe can only be tedious to you. Know that my friends were snatched away one by one, and I was left desolate. My own strength is exhausted, and I must tell, in a few words, what remains of my hideous narrative. I arrived in Geneva. My father and Ernest still lived, but my father sank under the news I brought. I see him now, excellent and venerable old man! His eyes wandered vacantly, for they had lost their charm and delight – his Elizabeth, more than a daughter to him. He loved her with all the affection a man feels, at the end of his life, when he has few affections remaining, and clings more closely to those who are left. Cursed, cursed be the fiend who brought misery upon his grey hairs, and caused him to decline in wretchedness! He could not withstand the horrors that had accumulated around him. The spring of his existence suddenly gave way, and he was unable to rise from his bed. He died a few days later in my arms.

What became of me? I don't know. I lost sensation, and chains and darkness were the only things I could feel pressing on me. Sometimes I dreamed that I wandered through flowery meadows and pleasant valleys with my childhood friends, but I awoke and found myself in a dungeon. Depression followed, but I gradually came to understand my situation, and my unhappiness. I was released from my prison. They had considered me insane, and I had lived for many months in solitary confinement.

Liberty would have been a useless gift to me, if I had not recovered my desire for revenge at the same time that I recovered my reason. As I remembered my past misfortunes, I began to reflect on their cause – the monster whom I had created, whom I had sent out into the world for my destruction. I was possessed by maddening rage when I thought about him. I wished, I prayed that I might have him within my grasp so that I could destroy him completely.

I did not confine my hate to useless wishes. I considered the best way to capture him. About a month after my release, I went to a criminal judge in the town and told him I had an accusation to make. I knew who had destroyed my family, and I requested him to use his full authority to capture the murderer. The magistrate listened to me with kindness and attention.

"Be assured, sir," he said, "I will do everything I can to find the villain."

"Thank you," I replied. "Listen to the story I have to tell. The tale is so strange, I might fear you will not believe it, except there is something in the truth that forces belief. The story includes too much detail to be my imagination, and I have no reason to lie." My manner as I spoke to him was steady and calm. I had determined to pursue my destroyer to the death, and this resolution quieted my agony and reconciled me to life for the time being. I told him briefly about my history, firmly and precisely, reporting the dates with accuracy and never becoming excited.

The magistrate appeared astonished at first, but as I continued to speak be became more interested and attentive. I saw him shudder with horror at times, and sometimes I saw surprise, though not disbelief, expressed on his face. When I had finished my story, I said, "I accuse this being, and call on you to use your power to seize and punish him. It is your duty as a magistrate, and I hope that your feelings as a man will not prevent you from carrying out your duty in this case.' My request caused considerable change in his expression. He had listened to my story with the kind of half-belief given to ghost stories or tales about supernatural events. But, when I asked him to act in his official capacity, his skepticism returned. He answered mildly, saying, "I would be glad to help you in your pursuit, but the creature you describe seems to have powers which would make my efforts useless. Who can follow an animal which can cross the sea of ice and lives in caves where no man can go? Besides, some months have passed since he committed his crimes, and it would be hard to guess where he might have wandered, or where he might live now."

"I am certain he lingers near the spot where I live. If he has taken refuge in the Alps, he can be hunted like the antelope and destroyed like a beast of prey. But, I can see your thoughts, you do not believe my story. You do not intend to pursue my enemy with the punishment he deserves."

My eyes sparkled with rage as I spoke, and the magistrate seemed intimidated. "You are mistaken,' he said. "If it is possible to seize this monster, he will be punished for his crimes. But, I am afraid from your description, it will not be possible.

We will make every effort, but you should prepare yourself for disappointment."

"That is impossible, but there is nothing I can say to convince you. My revenge means nothing to you. While I admit that revenge is wrong, it is the only passion that remains in my soul. I cannot contain my rage when I consider that the murderer I let loose upon the world still lives. You refuse my just demand. I have only one choice. I must commit myself, whether in life or death, to his destruction.

I trembled with agitation, and spoke in a frenzied manner, but I had the haughty fierceness of the ancient martyrs. The Genevan magistrate felt that my state of mind expressed madness, rather than devotion or heroism. He tried to soothe me as a nurse tries to soothe a child, and regarded my story as the result of delirium.

"Man,' I cried. 'You think you are wise! Stop, you do not know what you say."

I left the house, angry and disturbed, and withdrew to plan some other action.

Chapter 24

In my present situation, all rational thought was lost and swallowed up by fury. Revenge gave me focus and strength. It shaped my feelings and allowed me to be calm and calculating at times when delirium or death might have been my fate

My first decision was to leave Geneva forever. I had loved my country while I was happy and beloved, but it had become hateful to me. I supplied myself with a sum of money, and a few jewels that had belonged to my mother, and I left.

Now my wanderings began, which will continue as long as I live. I have traveled over a vast portion of the earth. I have endured all the hardships of traveling through deserts and barbarous countries. I hardly know how I have stayed alive. Many times I have stretched my failing limbs on the sandy plain and prayed for death. But, revenge kept me alive. I would not die and leave my enemy alive.

When I left Geneva, my first task was to find some clue so that I could trace the steps of my fiendish enemy. But, my plan was uncertain, and I wandered for many hours around the outskirts of the town, not knowing which way to go. As night approached, I found myself at the entrance of the cemetery where William, Elizabeth, and my father rested. I entered the cemetery and approached the tomb which marked their graves. Everything was silent, except for the leaves which blew gently in the wind. The night was dark, and the scene was solemn and impressive. The spirits of the departed seemed to flit around and cast a shadow, which the mourner could feel but not see.

The deep grief which this scene inspired quickly changed into rage and despair. They were dead, and I lived. Their murderer also lived. I must prolong my weary existence in order to destroy him. I knelt on the grass and kissed the earth. With trembling lips, I exclaimed, "By the sacred earth where I kneel, by the ghosts that wander near me, by the deep and eternal grief I feel, by the spirits that rule over the Night, I swear that I will pursue the demon who caused this misery. Either he or I will perish in mortal conflict. I will preserve my life for this purpose. I will behold the sun and walk upon the earth, so that I can carry out this revenge, otherwise these sights would vanish from my eyes forever. I call upon you, spirits of the dead, and I call on you, wandering ministers of vengeance, to guide me in my work. Let the cursed and hellish monster drink deep of agony. Let him feel the despair that now torments me."

I had begun my declaration solemnly. I almost felt that my murdered family heard and approved my promise. But, the furies possessed me as I finished speaking, and rage choked my words.

Through the stillness of the night, I was answered by a loud, fiendish laugh. It rang in my ears, long and heavy, and the mountains echoed with it. I would have destroyed my miserable existence in that moment, except that I had committed my life to vengeance. The laughter died away, and then a hated, familiar voice spoke close to my ear. He said in a whisper, "Miserable wretch, I am satisfied! You have determined to live, and I am satisfied."

I darted in the direction of his voice, but the devil eluded my grasp. Suddenly, the broad disk of the moon rose and shone full upon his ghastly, distorted shape as he fled at superhuman speed.

For many months, it has been my task to pursue him. I followed the windings of the Rhone River in vain. I reached the blue Mediterranean. One night, I happened to see the fiend, hiding himself on a ship bound for the Black Sea. I took passage on the same ship, but somehow he escaped.

I have followed his track through the wilds of Tartary and Russia, though he continued to evade me. Sometimes the peasants told me where he had gone, frightened of this horrid apparition. Sometimes he left some mark to guide me, afraid that I would despair and die if I lost all trace of him. The snows fell, and I saw the print of his huge foot on the white plain. You are just beginning life. You have not experienced agony and care. How can you understand what I have felt and still feel? Cold, hunger, and fatigue were the least part of the suffering I endured. I was cursed by some devil, and I carried eternal hell with me. Yet, a spirit of good still followed and directed my steps, and saved me from seemingly insurmountable difficulties when I was most in need. Sometimes, when I sank under exhaustion, overcome by hunger, a meal was prepared for me in the desert that restored and revived me. The food was plain, such as the peasants in the country ate, but I do not doubt it was put there by the spirits I had called upon to help me. Often, when everything was dry, the sky was cloudless and I was parched by thirst, a slight cloud would dim the sky, bringing rain that would revive me, and vanish.

I followed the course of the rivers when I could, but the demon generally avoided the rivers since many people lived there. In some places, I saw few human beings, and I subsisted on the wild animals that crossed my path. I gained the friendship of the villagers by distributing the money I had brought, or I would share some food I had killed. After taking a small part for myself, I would divide the rest with the people who gave me fire and utensils for cooking.

My life was hateful to me, and only during sleep did I taste joy. O blessed sleep! Often, when I was miserable, I sank into repose and my dreams lulled me into a state of delight. The spirits that guarded me provided me with these hours of happiness so that I could maintain my strength and fulfill my quest. Without this respite, I would have sunk under my hardships. During the day, I was sustained by the hope of night. While I slept, I saw my family, my wife, my beloved country. I saw the kind face of my father, and heard the silver voice of my Elizabeth. I saw Clerval enjoying health and youth. Often, when I was weary from a tiring march, I would tell myself that I was dreaming until night came and then I would enjoy reality in the arms of my dear family. I loved them with agonizing fondness. I clung to their dear forms, and sometimes they even haunted my waking hours. I would persuade myself that they still lived! At such moments, the vengeance that burned within me died in my heart. I pursued my path towards the destruction of the demon as a task assigned to me by heaven, the mechanical impulse of some unseen power, rather than the passionate desire of my soul. I cannot know the feelings of the being I pursed. Sometimes he left marks in writing on the bark of trees, or cut in the stone, that guided me and roused my fury. "My reign is not yet over" – these words were legible in one of the inscriptions – "You live, and my power is complete. Follow me, I seek the everlasting ice of the north. You will feel the misery of cold and frost, which do not bother me. If you do not delay too long, you will find a dead rabbit nearby, eat and be refreshed. Come, my enemy, we have yet to wrestle for our lives. You must still endure many hard, miserable hours until that time comes."

The devil was making fun of me! I renewed my vow of vengeance. I promised the miserable fiend torture and death. I would never give up my search until he or I should perish, and then I would joyfully rejoin Elizabeth and my departed family. Even now, they were preparing the reward for my tedious labor and horrible pilgrimage.

As I continued my journey northward, the snows grew deeper, and the cold increased until it was almost unbearable. The peasants were shut up in their hovels. Only the strongest ventured forth to seize the animals which were forced from their hiding places by starvation. The rivers were covered with ice, and it was impossible to get fish, so I was cut off from my chief sustenance. My enemy's triumph increased the more I had to suffer. One inscription that he left said, "Prepare! Your hardship is just beginning. Wrap yourself in furs and provide yourself with food. We will soon begin a journey where your suffering will satisfy my everlasting hatred."

My courage and perseverance were roused by this ridicule. I resolved not to fail in my purpose. Calling on heaven to support me, I continued across the immense distances, with unabated energy, until the ocean appeared on the horizon. It was so different from the blue seas of the south! The water was covered with ice, and it was more wild and rugged than the land. The Greeks wept with joy when they viewed the Mediterranean from the hills of Asia. I did not weep, but I knelt and thanked my guiding spirit with a full heart for bringing me safely to the place where I hoped to meet and struggle with my enemy.

Some weeks before, I had acquired a sledge and dogs, and thus I traveled over the snow at great speed. I do not know whether the fiend traveled the same way, but I started to catch up with him. Earlier, I had seemed to fall farther behind each day. When I first saw the ocean, he was just one day's journey ahead of me. I hoped to intercept him before he reached the beach. I pressed onward with renewed courage, and two days later I arrived at a wretched hamlet on the seashore. I asked the inhabitants for information about the fiend. They told me that a gigantic monster had arrived the night before armed with a gun and many pistols. His terrible appearance had frightened away the inhabitants of a solitary cottage. He had taken their store of winter food, carrying it away on a sledge pulled by numerous trained dogs. The horror-struck villagers were overjoyed that he had left the same night, continuing his journey across the sea in a direction that led to no land. They guessed that he would soon be destroyed by the breaking of the ice, or frozen by the eternal frost.

I felt sudden despair when I heard this news. He had escaped me, and I must undertake a destructive, endless journey across the mountainous ice that covered the ocean. The cold was so intense that few of the inhabitants could endure it for long. I came from a pleasant, sunny climate, and I could not hope to survive. Yet, my rage and vengeance returned when I considered that the fiend might live and be triumphant. It overwhelmed every other feeling like a mighty tide. While I took a short rest, the spirits of the dead hovered around and inspired me to strive for revenge. I prepared for the journey, exchanging my land-sledge for one more suited to the uneven surface of the frozen ocean. I purchased a plentiful stock of supplies and departed from the land.

I do not know how many days have passed since that time. I have endured misery which only the desire for just revenge, burning in my heart, allowed me to survive. Immense, rugged mountains of ice often barred my way. I often heard the thunder of breaking ice which threatened my destruction. But, the frost would return and make the paths of the sea secure.

Judging from the provisions I consumed, I would guess that I spent three weeks on this journey. The constant disappointment caused me to weep bitter tears. Despair nearly overwhelmed me. Once, the poor dogs expended incredible effort to reach the summit of a sloping ice mountain. Sinking under his fatigue, one of the dogs died, and I viewed the expanse

176

in front of me with anguish. Suddenly, my eye caught sight of a dark speck on the dusky plain. I strained my sight to distinguish what it could be, and uttered a wild cry of ecstasy when I recognized a sledge and the distorted proportions of the well-known figure within it. Oh! A burning gush of hope filled my heart. My eyes filled with warm tears, which I quickly wiped away. I wanted to keep the demon in sight. But, my vision was dimmed by burning tears as I gave way to the emotion that overwhelmed me and I wept out loud.

It was not the time for delay. I released the dogs from the harness that joined them to their dead companion, and gave them a plentiful portion of food. I let them rest for one hour, which was absolutely necessary, although it was bitterly irksome to me, and then I continued on my way. The sledge was still visible, and I did not lose sight of it, except when some ice-rock concealed it temporarily from view. Gradually, I gained on it. After two days' journey, I saw that my enemy was no more than one mile distant, and my heart bounded within me.

But, just when my foe seemed within my grasp, my hopes were suddenly extinguished. I lost all trace of him, more completely than I had ever done before. I could hear the thunder of ice breaking, and the waters rolled and swelled beneath me. The sound became more ominous and terrible every moment. I pressed onward, but in vain. The wind rose, and the sea roared. With a mighty shock, similar to an earthquake, the ice split and cracked with a tremendous, overwhelming sound. Within a few minutes, a tumultuous sea rolled between me and my enemy. I was left drifting on a shattered piece of ice that continuously shrank and brought me closer to a hideous death. Many appalling hours passed in this way. Several of my dogs died, and I myself was about to sink under the distress, when I saw your ship riding at anchor. It gave me hope of rescue and life. I had no idea that ships ever came so far north, and I was astonished at the sight. I quickly destroyed part of my sledge to use as oars, and with great effort I moved my ice raft in the direction of your ship. I had decided, if you were traveling southward, I would trust myself to the mercy of the sea, rather than abandon my purpose. I hoped to persuade you to give me a boat so that I could pursue my enemy. But, you were traveling northwards. You took me on board when my energy was exhausted. Overwhelmed by many hardships, I should soon have faced the death that I still dread, for my task is not finished.

Oh! When will my guiding spirit bring me to the demon and allow me to rest? Or, must I die while he still lives? If I die, swear to me, Walton, he will not escape. You will seek him and satisfy my vengeance in his death. Do I dare ask you to undertake my pilgrimage and suffer the hardships that I have undergone? No, I am not so selfish. But, when I am dead, if he should appear, if the ministers of vengeance should bring him to you, swear that he will not live. Swear that he will not triumph over my misfortunes and survive to increase the number of his crimes. He is eloquent and persuasive, and once his words had power over my heart. But, do not trust him. His soul is as hellish as his fiendish form, full of treachery and malice. Do not listen to him. Call on the names of William, Justine, Clerval, Elizabeth, my father, and the wretched Victor, and thrust your sword into his heart. My spirit will hover nearby and direct the blade.

Walton, continued –
August 26th, 17—

You have read this strange and terrible story, Margaret. Do you feel your blood congeal with horror as mine does now? Sometimes, seized by sudden agony, he could not continue his story. At other times, he spoke with difficulty. His voice was broken, but piercing, and the words were filled with anguish. At times, his fine, lovely eyes were lighted with indignation, and other times they were subdued by sorrow and quenched by infinite wretchedness. Sometimes, he could control his tone and expression, and he would describe the most horrible incidents in a calm voice. He would suppress every trace of agitation, until his face suddenly changed into an expression of the wildest rage as he shrieked out curses against his persecutor.

His story is logical, and it carries the appearance of simple truth. Yet, I must confess that I was more convinced by the letters of Felix and Safie, which he showed me and the appearance of the monster seen from our own ship, than I was by his story, no matter how logical and earnest he seemed. Such a monster really exists! I cannot doubt it, but I am stunned and amazed. Sometimes, I tried to question Frankenstein about the details of his creature's formation. But, he would not speak about this point.

"Are you mad, my friend?" he said. "Where would your senseless curiosity lead you? Would you create, like me, a demon-like enemy for yourself and the world? Peace, peace! Learn from my misery, and do not seek to increase your own."

Frankenstein discovered that I was making notes about his story. He asked to see the notes and made corrections himself, adding to the notes in many places. In particular, he gave life and spirit to the conversations he held with his enemy.

"Since you have recorded my story," he said, "I would like the record to be accurate."

One week had passed away while I listened to the strangest story that could be imagined. My thoughts and feelings have been absorbed by interest for my guest, both due to his story and his own refined, gentle manners. I wish to comfort him, but can I counsel him to live, when he is so infinitely miserable, and he has lost every hope of consolation? Oh, no! He will only be happy when he composes his shattered spirit to embrace peace and death. Yet, he enjoys one comfort which is the result of his solitude and delirium. He believes that when he dreams he speaks with his family. From that communion he gains comfort for his miseries or inspiration for his vengeance. He believes the beings themselves visit him from some remote world, and they are not simply the creations of his imagination. This faith gives his reflections a solemnity that makes them as interesting and imposing as truth.

Our conversations are not restricted to his own history and misfortunes. He displays unbounded knowledge and keen understanding about every aspect of general literature. His eloquence is forceful. I cannot hear him speak about pity or love, or describe some pathetic incident, without being moved to tears. What a glorious creature he must have been in his happier days, when he seems so noble and godlike in his ruin! He seems to understand his own worth, and the greatness of his fall.

"When I was young," he said, "I believed that I was destined for some great enterprise. While my feelings are deep, I had a coolness of judgment that fitted me for great achievement. Knowing my own worth supported me when others might have become discouraged. I considered it criminal to throw away my talent in useless grief when I might do something useful for my fellow creatures. I did not consider the creation of a sensitive, rational animal to be a common achievement. This thought lifted me up at the beginning of my work, but now it only makes me lower than the dust. All my speculations and hopes have come to nothing. Like the archangel who wished to be godlike, I am chained in an eternal hell. I had a vivid imagination combined with the ability to think critically and apply myself intensely. Using my abilities, I conceived the idea and executed the plan for creation of a man. Even now, it excites me when I recall my thoughts before the work was finished. My thoughts rose higher than the skies. I exulted in my powers, and burned with the idea of what I would achieve. From childhood, I was filled with high hopes and lofty ambition. But, how I am sunk! My friend, if you had known me as I used to be, you would not recognize me in this degraded state. High destiny seemed to carry me onward, and my heart rarely felt despair, until I fell, never, never to rise again!"

Must I lose this admirable being? I have longed for a friend. I have searched for one who would sympathize and care for me. Behold, I have found such a friend on these desert seas. But, I fear that I have gained him only to realize his value and lose him. I would make him wish to live again, but he rejects the idea.

"I thank you, Walton," he said, "for caring what happens to such a miserable wretch. But, when you talk about new ties and fresh affections, do you think anyone can replace those who are gone? Can I care for any man as I did for Clerval, or love any woman as I loved Elizabeth? The friends we knew in childhood always have power over our minds, even when the affections are not based on any special qualities. They know our childhood nature, which we always retain, no matter how it changes later, and they understand our actions. Siblings trust each other, unless they have early experience to the contrary. Friends can distrust one another, no matter how strongly they are attached. I have had friends whom I loved not only from habit

181

and association but because of their own merits. Wherever I might be, I will always hear the conversation of Clerval, and the soothing voice of Elizabeth. They are dead. In my loneliness, only one feeling could persuade me to preserve my life. If I was engaged in some important work or project which might benefit my fellow creatures, then I might live to fulfill it. But, such is not my destiny. I must pursue and destroy the being I brought to life. Then, my fate on earth will be fulfilled, and I may die."

September 2nd
My beloved Sister,

I am surrounded by danger as I write to you. I do not know whether I will ever again see England and the dear friends who live there. I am surrounded by mountains of ice which allow no escape, and threaten to crush my ship every instant. The brave fellows whom I have persuaded to be my companions look to me for help, but I have none to give. Our situation is terribly appalling, but I have not lost my hope and courage. Yet, it is terrible to know that I have put the lives of all these men in danger. If we are lost, my mad schemes are the reason.

What must you be thinking, Margaret? You will not know that I have perished, and you will wait anxiously for my return. Years will pass, and you will feel despair, and yet you will be tortured by hope. Oh! My beloved sister, the sickening failure of your hope seems more terrible to me than my own death.

But, you have a husband and lovely children, and you may be happy. Heaven bless you, and make you so!

My unfortunate guest regards me with compassion. He tries to give me hope, and he speaks as if life was something he valued. He reminds me how often such accidents have happened to others who have tried to sail this sea. He fills me

with cheerful hope about the future, in spite of myself. Even the
sailors feel the power of his eloquence. When he speaks, they
no longer feel despair. He rouses their energy. While they hear
his voice, they believe that these vast mountains of ice are mole-
hills, and they will vanish when confronted by human
determination. These feelings are fleeting. Their fears increase
each day that hope is delayed. I almost dread a mutiny caused
by this despair.

September 5th
        Something has happened so interesting, that I cannot
help recording it, even though it is likely these pages will never
reach you.
        We are still surrounded by mountains of ice, and we are
still in imminent danger of being crushed as they collide. The
cold is extreme, and many of my unfortunate comrades have
already perished amidst this scene of desolation. Frankenstein's
health has declined each day. A feverish fire still glimmers in his
eyes, but he is exhausted. He sinks into apparent lifelessness
when he is roused by any sudden exertion.
        In my last letter, I mentioned my fear of mutiny. This
morning I sat looking at my friend's pale face – his eyes half-
closed and his arms hanging listlessly – when I was roused by half
a dozen sailors who demanded entrance to the cabin. They
entered, and their leader addressed me. They told me that the
other sailors had chosen them to make a request which, in
fairness, I could not refuse. We were trapped by ice and would
probably never escape. But, they were afraid that if the ice did
dissipate and free passage should open, I would still want to
continue my voyage and lead them into new dangers, just when
they had escaped from this one. They wanted me to promise

that if the vessel should be freed, I would immediately direct my course southwards.

This speech troubled me. I had not yet despaired, nor had I determined to return if we were set free. Yet, could I, in fairness, refuse this demand? Would it be possible to refuse? I hesitated before I answered. Frankenstein had been silent at first, seeming too weak even to attend. Now he roused himself, his eyes sparkled, and his cheeks flushed with momentary vigor. He turned towards the men and said, "What do you mean? What do you demand from your captain? Do you give up so easily? Did you not call this a glorious expedition?

Why was it glorious? Not because the way was smooth and peaceful as the southern sea, but because it was full of danger and terror, because your courage and strength would be tested by every new incident. Danger and death would surround you, and you would brave them, and overcome them. This made your undertaking honorable and glorious. History would regard you as benefactors of humankind. Your names would be respected as men who had bravely faced death for the honor and benefit of humanity. Now, behold, with the first inkling of danger, the first mighty trial of your courage, you shrink away. You are content to be remembered as men who did not have the strength to endure cold and danger. Poor souls, they were chilly, and returned to their warm firesides. That did not require all this effort. You did not need to come this far, and drag your captain through the shame of defeat, simply to prove yourselves cowards. Oh! Be men, or be more than men. Be steady to your purpose, and firm as a rock. This ice is not stronger than your hearts might be. It cannot withstand you, if you determine that it shall not. Do not return to your families with the shame of disgrace marked upon you. Return as heroes who have fought and conquered, and did not turn their backs on the enemy."

His voice was so expressive, his eyes so full of lofty feeling and heroism, can you wonder that the men were moved? They looked at one another, and they could not reply. I spoke and told them to consider what they had heard. I would not lead them farther north if they strongly opposed it, but I hoped that, with reflection, their courage would return. They left the room, and I turned towards my friend, but he had sunk into languor, and almost appeared lifeless.

I do not know how all this will end. But, I would rather die than return in shame without fulfilling my purpose. Yet, I fear that this will be my fate. Unsupported by ideas of glory and honor, the men cannot continue to endure their present hardships.

September 7th

The die is cast. I have agreed to return if we are not destroyed. My hopes are blasted by cowardice and indecision. I will return disappointed and ignorant of any new discovery. I am hardly able to bear this injustice with patience.

September 12th

It is over. I am returning to England. I have lost my dreams of usefulness and glory. I have lost my friend. But, I will try to describe these bitter events to you, my dear sister, and while I am returning to England, and to you, I will not despair.

September 9th, the ice began to move, and roaring like thunder was heard in the distance as the islands split and cracked in every direction. We were in imminent peril, but we could do nothing but wait. My attention remained focused on my unfortunate guest. His illness had increased to such a degree that he could not leave his bed. The ice cracked behind us, and it was driven towards the north. A breeze sprang up from the west, and on the 11th the passage towards the south became perfectly free. When the sailors saw that their return home seemed assured, a loud, tumultuous shout of joy broke from them. Frankenstein, who was dozing, awoke and asked about the noise. I said, "They shout because they will soon return to England."

"Do you really return?"

"Alas! Yes, I cannot oppose their demands. I cannot lead them into danger if they are unwilling, and I must return."

"Do so if you choose, but I will not. You may give up your purpose, but my task is assigned to me by heaven, and I dare not give it up. I am weak, but surely the spirits who support my vengeance will give me strength." He tried to rise from the bed as he spoke, but the effort was too much for him, and he fell back and fainted.

It was a long time before he regained consciousness. I often thought that his life was extinguished. When he finally opened his eyes, he had difficulty breathing and could not speak. The doctor gave him medicine and ordered us not to disturb him. He told me that my friend did not have many hours to live.

After the sentence was pronounced, I could only grieve and be patient. I sat by his bed, watching him. His eyes were closed, and I thought he slept. But, after some time he called to me in a weak voice and asked me to come closer. "Alas!" he said. "The strength that I relied on is gone. I feel that I will soon die, and he, my enemy and persecutor, will still be alive. Do not imagine, Walton, that in my last moments I still feel that burning hatred and passionate desire for revenge that I once expressed. But, I feel justified in wishing for the death of my adversary. I have spent these last days thinking back over my actions, and I do not find myself to blame. In a fit of enthusiastic madness, I created a rational creature. It was my duty to assure his happiness and well-being, as far as it was in my power.

This was my duty, but I had a greater responsibility, which was my duty towards the members of my own species. I was right to refuse the request to create a companion for the first creature. He demonstrated his evil and selfishness. He destroyed my family. He devoted himself to the destruction of beings who possessed exquisite feelings, happiness, and wisdom. I do not know where his thirst for vengeance will end. He is miserable himself, and he should die so that he does not make others miserable. It was my task to destroy him, but I have failed. I was motivated by selfish, vicious feelings when I asked you to undertake my unfinished work. I ask you again now, but I am motivated only by reason and virtue.

Yet, I cannot ask you to renounce your family and country to fulfill this task. Now that you are returning to England, you will have little chance of meeting him. But, I will leave it to you to determine what you should do. My judgment and thoughts are affected by the near approach of death. I will not ask you to do what I think is best, because I might be mistaken.

It disturbs me to think that he should live and continue to do evil deeds. Otherwise, this hour is the happiest I have known for several years. I expect death to come at any moment and bring me release. I can see the forms of my beloved dead, and I hurry into their arms. Farewell, Walton! Seek happiness in peace. Avoid ambition, even if it is the seemingly innocent ambition of scientific discovery. Yet, why do I say this? I have been blasted in my hopes, but others may succeed."

His voice became fainter as he spoke, and he gradually sank into silence, exhausted by his effort. About half an hour later, he tried to speak again, but he could not. He pressed my hand weakly, and his eyes closed forever. A gentle smile faded from his lips.

Margaret, what can I say about the untimely passing of this generous spirit? What can I say that will make you understand the depth of my sorrow? My words would seem feeble and inadequate. My tears flow, and my mind is overshadowed by disappointment. But, I journey towards England, and I may find comfort there.

I am interrupted by a noise. What does it mean? It is midnight, and there is a fair breeze. The men watching on deck scarcely move. Again, there is a sound like a hoarse human voice. It comes from the cabin where the remains of Frankenstein still lie. I must go and investigate. Good night, my sister.

Great God! What a scene has just taken place! The memory still makes my head spin. I hardly know whether I have the power to describe it. Yet, the story I have recorded would be incomplete without this final chapter. I entered the cabin where lay the remains of my unfortunate, admirable friend. A gigantic form with distorted proportions leaned over him. His face was hidden by long locks of ragged black hair as he leaned over the coffin. The figure extended one vast hand which resembled the color and texture of a mummy. When he heard me approach, he stopped uttering exclamations of grief and horror and sprang towards the window. I have never seen anything as horrible as his loathsome, appalling face. I shut my eyes involuntarily, and tried to consider what I should do. I called him back.

He paused and looked at me with wonder. As he turned towards the lifeless form of his creator, he seemed to forget my presence. Every feature and gesture seemed suffused by some wild, uncontrollable feeling.

"That is also my victim!" he exclaimed. "My crimes are consummated by his murder. The miserable course of my life has come to an end. Oh, Frankenstein! Generous, self-devoted being! It does not matter now that I ask you to forgive me. I have destroyed him by destroying everything he loved. Alas! He is cold, and he cannot answer me." His voice sounded choked. My first impulse was to obey the dying request of my friend, and fulfill my duty by destroying his enemy. A mixture of curiosity and compassion prevented me. I approached this tremendous being. I did not dare to raise my eyes again and look at his face, there was something so frightening and unearthly in his ugliness. I tried to speak, but the words died away on my lips. The monster continued to utter wild, incoherent self-reproaches. I finally gathered the resolve to speak to him during a pause in his storm of feeling.

"Your repentance does not matter now," I said. "If you had listened to the voice of conscience and obeyed the stings of remorse before your diabolical vengeance reached this point, Frankenstein would still be alive."

"Do you imagine," the demon said, "do you think I did not feel agony and remorse?" He pointed to the corpse and said, "He did not suffer when the deed was done. Oh! He did not suffer one ten-thousandth of the anguish I felt during the slow execution of the deed. A frightful selfishness pushed me on, while my heart was poisoned by remorse. Do you think I enjoyed hearing the groans of Clerval? My heart was formed for love and sympathy. When misery turned my heart to hatred and vice, the change involved torture that you cannot even imagine.

After Clerval's murder, I returned to Switzerland, heart-broken and overcome by pity. My pity for Frankenstein amounted to horror. I hated myself. Then I discovered that he dared to hope for happiness while he heaped wretchedness and despair upon me. He was the source of my existence, and the cause of my unspeakable torment. He sought his own enjoyment in feelings and passions from which I was barred forever.

Impotent envy and bitter indignation filled me with a thirst for vengeance that could not be satisfied. I remembered my threat and resolved to carry it out. I knew that I was preparing deadly torture for myself. But, I was the slave, not the master, of an impulse which I hated but I could not disobey. Yet, I was not miserable when she died. I had pushed away all feeling, subdued all anguish, to revel in my extreme despair. From that time, evil became my good. Having gone so far, I was forced to adapt my nature to the design I had willingly chosen. The fulfillment of my plan was driven by passion that I could not resist. Now it is ended, and there is my last victim!"

At first I was touched by his expressions of misery, but I remembered what Frankenstein had said about his powers of eloquence and persuasion. Indignation kindled within me when I looked at the lifeless form of my friend. "Wretch!" I said. "You have come here to whine over the desolation which you have caused. You have thrown a torch onto a pile of buildings, and after they are consumed you sit among the ruins and lament the fall. Hypocritical fiend! If the man you mourn still lived, he would still be the object of your accursed vengeance. You do not feel pity. You are only sorry that your victim has withdrawn beyond your evil power."

"Oh, it is not true – not true," the being interrupted. "Yet my actions must have given you this impression. I do not seek compassion in my misery. I will never find sympathy. When I first looked for sympathy, my whole being overflowed with love of virtue and feelings of happiness and affection that I wanted to share. But, now virtue has become like a shadow to me, and happiness and affection have turned into bitter loathing and despair. Where would I find sympathy? I am content to suffer alone, as long as my sufferings continue. I accept that when I die I will be remembered with hatred. Once I dreamed of virtue, and fame, and enjoyment. Once I falsely hoped to meet beings who would overlook my outward form, and love me for the excellent qualities I was capable of developing. I was nourished with lofty thoughts of honor and devotion. But, now crime had degraded me beneath the lowest animal. No guilt, no evil, no misery can compare with mine. When I consider the frightful list of my sins, I cannot believe that I am the same creature whose thoughts were once filled with sublime, transcendent visions of beauty, and the majesty of goodness. But, it is so. The fallen angel becomes the devil. Yet, even the devil had friends and associates in his desolation. I am alone.

You call Frankenstein your friend, and you seem to know about my crimes and his misfortunes. But, when he told you about them, he could not describe the hours and months of misery I endured, consumed by impotent passion. While I destroyed his hopes, I did not satisfy my own desires. My feelings remained forever ardent and unsatisfied. I still desired love and friendship, and I was still rejected. Was there no injustice in this? Should I be considered the only criminal, when all humankind sinned against me? Why do you not hate Felix, who drove his friend from his door with hatred? Why do you not condemn the peasant who tried to destroy the person who saved his child? No, they are considered pure, virtuous beings! I am abandoned and miserable, and I am considered something to trampled and kicked, spurned and rejected. Even now, my blood boils when I think about this injustice.

But, it is true that I am a wretch. I have murdered the lovely and the helpless. I have strangled the innocent as they slept, and choked to death people who had never hurt me or any other living being. My creator was worthy of love and admiration, and I have condemned him to misery. I have pursued him to his final ruin.

There he lies, white and cold in death. You hate me, but you cannot hate me as much as I hate myself. I look at the hands which carried out the deed. I consider the heart that conceived the idea, and I long for the moment when these hands will cover my eyes, and that vision will no longer haunt my thoughts.

Do not worry that I will commit some evil action in the future. My work is nearly complete. I do not require your death, or any man's death, to complete my life and accomplish what must be done. But, I do require my own death. Do not imagine that I will be slow to perform this sacrifice. I will leave your ship on the ice raft that brought me here. I will travel as far north as I can go. I will collect my funeral pyre and consume this miserable frame to ashes. Nothing will remain that might encourage some curious, unhallowed wretch to create another being like me. I will die. I will no longer feel the agony that consumes me, I will not be prey to feelings that will never be satisfied. The man who created me is dead, and when I die, we will soon be forgotten. I will no longer see the sun or stars or feel the wind on my cheeks.

Light, sense, and feeling will pass away, and in that state I must find happiness. When I first beheld this world, some years ago, when I felt the cheerfulness of summer and heard the rustling of leaves and the warbling of birds, they were everything to me, and I would have wept to die. Now death is my only consolation. Polluted by crimes, and torn by bitter remorse, where can I find rest except in death?

Farewell! You are the last human being I will ever see. Farewell, Frankenstein! If you were still alive, and you still desired revenge, my life would satisfy you better than my death. But, you wanted to destroy me, so I would not commit more evil actions. You could not desire vengeance against me greater than I feel myself. Blasted as you were, my agony was greater than yours. The bitter sting of remorse will rankle in my wounds until death closes them forever."

With sad, solemn enthusiasm, he cried, "I will die soon. I will no longer feel as I do now. Soon this burning misery will be extinguished. I will climb my funeral pyre in triumph, and glory in the torture of the flames. The light of that fire will fade away, and the winds will sweep my ashes into the sea. My spirit will sleep in peace, or if it thinks, it surely will not think as it does now. Farewell."

As he spoke, he sprang from the cabin window onto the ice raft which lay close to the ship. He was soon carried away by the waves and lost in the darkness and distance.

∞∞∞∞∞∞∞∞∞∞∞∞∞∞∞∞∞∞∞∞∞